THE BONDS OF
MATRI-MONEY

THE BONDS OF MATRI-MONEY

•

Gina Ardito

AVALON BOOKS
NEW YORK

Published by Thomas Bouregy & Co., Inc.
160 Madison Avenue, New York, NY 10016

Library of Congress Cataloging-in-Publication Data

Ardito, Gina.
    The bonds of matri-money / Gina Ardito.
        p. cm.
    ISBN-13: 978-0-8034-9813-6 (acid-free paper)
    ISBN-10: 0-8034-9813-6 (acid-free paper)
    1. Married people—Fiction.   2. Reality television programs—
Fiction. I. Title.
    PS3601.R43B66 2007
    813'.6—dc22   2006029678

PRINTED IN THE UNITED STATES OF AMERICA
ON ACID-FREE PAPER
BY HADDON CRAFTSMEN, BLOOMSBURG, PENNSYLVANIA

For Philip, who shares my life, owns my heart, and makes every day a joy.
No one else could make these bonds so much fun.

Chapter One

"Of course we'll appeal the decision."

Inside a Manhattan civil courtroom, Renata Moon gripped the defense table's edge to keep from sinking to the floor in shock. Her nails dug into the mahogany veneer while the reality of the verdict sank in. Eighty-seven thousand dollars? It might as well be a million. Majestic Health Contractors was a fledgling nonprofit organization. They couldn't possibly afford to pay such an exorbitant sum.

"But . . . ?" She prompted the attorney to continue his statement. There was always a *but* when it came to attorneys, a protective cloak that exempted them from punishment when they miscalculated, regardless of the outcome to their clients.

The lawyer sighed then picked up his Coach bag. "*But,* it's going to cost a lot, and I'm not sure we'll get a more favorable decision in the end."

"I don't understand, Mr. Levy," Renata exclaimed, tying a knot in the ribbon of nausea in her stomach. "You said this was a frivolous lawsuit."

"I also told you I couldn't guarantee a jury would see it the same way. Juries are capricious by nature."

Beside Renata, her partner, Connell MacAllister, shoved a manila folder full of papers into a briefcase and snapped the locks closed. The click-click reverberated with the power of gunfire in the cavernous room.

"It's unbelievable," he said through whitened lips. "A guy on a construction site cuts his hand on a circular saw and winds up on disability. Bored at home while his wife's at work, he starts an online affair with a woman he meets in a chat room. Now our firm owes the soon-to-be-ex-wife eighty-seven thousand dollars?"

Mr. Levy shrugged. "Your firm should have anticipated the dangers associated with a circular saw."

Connell's eyes nearly rolled out of their sockets. "I hardly see how his incompetence with a power tool makes us liable for the break-up of their marriage."

"If not for the hand injury, he wouldn't have been home. If he hadn't been home, he wouldn't have found the chat room. If not for the chat room, he wouldn't have started an affair. That makes you liable. At least, that's how the jury saw it."

"So that's it? That's our day in court?" Connell retorted. "Why didn't the spurned woman sue the computer company? Or the owner of the chat room? How about the makers of the circular saw? While we're at it, have her sue Bill Gates. At least he can afford the hundred grand."

Mr. Levy's expression remained bland during Connell's tirade. "Like I said, we'll appeal." Shooting his cuffs, he picked up his leather bag and turned toward the exit. "I'll have Janine mail you a statement of charges thus far."

Renata watched him go, her eyes flinging daggers between his shoulder blades as he strode from the courtroom. Great. Today's decision had probably bankrupted them, and the great and powerful Mr. Levy thought of nothing but his billable hours. No wonder lawyers got a bad rap; sometimes, they deserved it.

Connell looked up from the paperwork littering his desk and met Renata's worried gaze. "It's hopeless."

"There has to be some way to save the organization."

"Not without a miracle."

She sank into the leather chair, the hiss of compressed air sounding like a sigh of defeat. "How big a miracle?"

"Does it matter?"

Renata winced, and he regretted allowing frustration to get the better of him. When her eyes glossed beneath unshed tears, his gut twisted with guilt. He'd known her for three years now and could not get used to those eyes. They communicated her every emotion.

She'd first come to him seeking a contractor to renovate an old ranch house, widening hallways and rooms to accommodate large medical equipment for a single mother of five who'd been diagnosed with lung cancer. The work had to be done quickly and with as little cost as possible since Renata planned to pay for it through charitable donations. He'd melted at the sight of her pleading golden-brown eyes. Not only had he agreed to take on the project, he'd found himself signing on as a permanent partner. All because of those eyes.

Shaken by the raw pain he saw there now, he dropped his gaze back to the ledger on his desk. "We've got a balloon payment due at the end of the month. And no bank will refinance us with the lawsuit decision sitting over our heads. On top of that, Marroneck Building Supply must have already heard about our little financial downturn. They won't send us so much as a two-by-four unless we're prepared to pay on delivery—cash."

"But the Bardonelli project," she sputtered. "The rainy April put us weeks behind on getting Chelsea's ramp erected. And I promised Mr. Bardonelli that ramp would be ready and decked out with a big pink ribbon when she's discharged from rehab."

"I hate to say it, but that's not going to happen."

Renata slammed her palm on his desk, fingers splaying across the numbers. "It has to. I'm not letting that poor family down. How much cash do we need to finish the Bardonelli job?"

"About ten grand, give or take. But Renata, we just plain don't have it. We've got other bills to pay and only about eight thousand left in cash reserve. And that's before we pay Mr. Levy for his stellar representation. There's simply no way we can raise enough money in charitable donations in such a short amount of time to stay afloat."

"What about your contracting firm? Can you swing a loan to tide us over?"

He shook his head. "I'm mortgaged to the hilt already. How about you? Got anything left on your credit union account?"

Her teeth bit into her lower lip. "Maxed. As is my 401(k) loan availability."

"Well, that's it then," he said on a defeated sigh. "Majestic Health Contractors is officially out of business."

"No. I can't accept that. I won't accept it. I'll call Marroneck and beg them to extend us more credit."

"It won't work."

"I've got a ten-year-old girl who's facing the rest of her life in a wheelchair due to a freak gymnastics accident. The least I can do is make sure her house is accessible to her when she comes home. I've got to try. This means too much to me."

It meant just as much to him, but he really didn't see any light at the end of this tunnel. Despite his fatalistic viewpoint, however, he offered her an encouraging smile. "Have at 'em, tiger. I'll go along with whatever you come up with."

Early the next morning, a bone-weary Renata managed to push herself the last few steps to her apartment and found a note taped to the center of the door:

Renata,
I've met someone else. Her name is Leyla. We just got married and moved to Rio. I'm really sorry but love happens when it happens.
Steve

She sighed. Another of her boyfriend's practical jokes. Crumpling the floral paper in her hand, she entered the apartment.

"Ha, ha, Steve, very funny," she called as she kicked off her shoes. "I'm really not in the mood. I could actually use a little TLC. We lost the case yesterday. Connell thinks we'll have to close the business."

Cutting off a limb with a rusty butter knife couldn't hurt as much as saying good-bye to the organization she had built from scratch. Still in its infancy at only three years old, Majestic Health Contractors would never live to reach adulthood now, thanks to the greed of some bitter, jilted woman in Glen Cove.

"Feel like helping me crunch some numbers?"

No answer came from the bedroom, and a flutter of unease tickled down her spine in direct rhythm to the drip-drip-drip of the leaky kitchen faucet.

"Steve?" A thud came from the bedroom, and she

released the breath she'd held. "I'm gonna make coffee. Want some?"

No answer. The drip-drips continued, now joined by an occasional thump. Despite her exhaustion, Renata smiled. The man had such a wicked sense of humor. She picked up her shoes and strode into the bedroom.

Strange. No Steve in sight. And the bed was made.

"C'mon, enough already." She saw no movement, no shadows, nothing to indicate where he might have hidden this time. Annoyance itched her skin. "This isn't funny."

When a guttural trill came from behind her, she whirled, ready to smack him with her shoes. "Aha!"

A high-pitched screech pierced her eardrums, and she screamed in reaction, dropping the shoes on her stocking feet. Her heartbeat thundered in her temples as she stared. Black eyes stared at her from a gray and white feathered face with round orange circles on its cheeks.

"Buttons!" she finally exclaimed. "How did you get in here?"

Buttons, her neighbor's pied cockatiel, chirped to explain her presence while flying onto Renata's shoulder.

"Uh-huh," she replied. "So where's Steve? Don't tell me you two switched places. I get to keep you and Lillian keeps him?"

The bird emitted an ear-ringing whistle, and Renata translated the noise to mean Buttons found the idea amusing.

"Well, you're not getting coffee." She rubbed a hand over the prickly yellowish pin feathers on Buttons' head. "You're hyper enough as it is."

With the cockatiel riding on her shoulder, she headed into the living room and flipped on the light. The unease of earlier deepened to apprehension. Every shred of evidence that Steve had ever lived in this apartment had been magically erased. Framed photographs, dog-eared sports posters, the ugly old lamp shaped like a beer bottle—all gone.

Numb now, she returned to the bedroom. Buttons took off from her shoulder and flew to the closet. Renata followed, her footsteps slow and heavy. Reality hit home the moment she yanked open the closet door. A row of naked clothes hangers on his side jangled against one another.

She would have sunk to her knees but a series of knocks sent her racing back to greet Lillian, the old lady who lived next door.

"Rennie," she said, peering inside, "did Buttons sneak past Steve when he had the door open earlier?"

"Y-you saw Steve today? When?"

Lillian nodded, causing the gold turban on her head to slip until it rested cockeyed over her left ear. "He left about an hour ago with an exotic-looking woman wearing a bright red bandeau and floral skirt." Her tongue clacked against her dentures. "Much too vibrant an ensemble for daytime. He introduced us. Now, let me think, what was her name again?"

"Leyla," she said with despair.

The old lady snapped her fingers. "Yes, that was it. Leyla Escobar. Who is she?"

In reply, Renata handed her the crumpled note.

"You mean, Steve is gone?"

A whirlwind of emotions choked Renata's throat. Anger, bitterness, fear, and misery all fought to reach the surface, and she swallowed them down with a large gulp then nodded.

"Thank God," Lillian said. "He didn't deserve you, Rennie. I kept telling you he'd break your heart in the end."

"I guess." She still couldn't get used to the idea. One word permeated the fog inside her brain: why?

"Well, good riddance to bad rubbish, I always say. So, now that I know my Buttons is safe, fill me in on what happened with your case yesterday."

Ah, yes, the more important tragedy on this Black Wednesday. Lillian was right. Concentrate on Chelsea Bardonelli, on all the Chelsea Bardonellis and their parents who would now find it more difficult and much more expensive to make their homes handicap accessible.

Briefly, she told Lillian about the trial, the jury's decision and the aftershocks, ending with Connell's opinion that their company couldn't survive.

Lillian paused a moment. "You know what? I just might have a solution for you. I'll be right back."

Chapter Two

A new game show entitled "The Bonds of Matrimoney" is seeking newlyweds in the tri-state area willing to spend a month in the South Pacific for the chance to win one million dollars . . .

Seated at her kitchen table, Renata looked up from the newspaper article and into her neighbor's heavily made-up face. "I can't do this."

"Of course you can," Lillian told her. "As a matter of fact, I'd say this game show is just what you need."

"Don't start that again. Please?" She wanted to push away from the table, but the old lady's cardinal talons dug into her wrist, pinning her in place.

"Start what?"

"That, 'you should take a risk now and then,' speech."

"Well, it's true. You've spent your whole life living by the rules, and what's it ever got you? Your closest friends are your Nana, Buttons and me—three useless, senile broads with more miles on them than Route 66." Buttons apparently took offense and screeched her outrage in near glass-breaking tones.

"Be quiet, old girl." Lillian passed the cockatiel a piece of corn muffin. "You and I may be ancient but we've still got our sex appeal. Rennie, honey, you need to shake up your life. Otherwise, you'll wind up an old lady all alone, wondering when your life passed you by."

"And you're the voice of experience?" she retorted. "You live all alone, except for Buttons."

"Yes, but I had a glorious time in my youth. Years ago, I had men clamoring to smell the perfume on my gloves."

"You did not."

Lillian nodded, tipping the gold turban forward over her forehead. "Indeed I did. Have I ever told you about the night I spent with Henry Kissinger?"

"No."

"Back in 1969, Henry was giving a speech at the U.N. and took in our Christmas show at Radio City Music Hall. Did you ever see one of those shows? With the live animals on stage during the Nativity scene? Do you have any idea how hard it is to maintain a straight kick line with two dozen other girls while you're all hopping up and down in camel dung?"

"But you digress . . ." Renata prompted, rolling her hands to speed up Lillian's memory.

"Yes, of course. How silly of me. Anyway, after the show, Henry sent a note backstage requesting my company for a late supper at the Russian Tea Room. Naturally, I went."

"Naturally."

"One doesn't say no to a Secretary of State."

"Yes, Miss Manners."

"We were sitting in a booth at the Tea Room, enjoying baklava of squab and making our way through a bottle of Cristal when all of a sudden, one of his people interrupted us. The CIA believed a major crisis would develop in Cambodia in the next week. Do you know what Henry said to his aide?"

"What?"

"Never taking his eyes off me, he said, 'There cannot be a crisis next week. My schedule is already full.' "

"You're making that up."

Lillian's grin widened. "No, I'm not. But regardless, you're missing my point. Your life is full of crises because you make time for them."

"That's a pretty simplistic view, don't you think?"

Lillian shrugged, causing Buttons to bounce up and down for a brief second. The cockatiel gave her owner a perturbed look, then settled down to nibble at her corn muffin again. "Simplistic or not, there's some truth to it. You need to do something proactive about this situation. Sitting here writing a list on a legal pad isn't going to get you the money you need."

"I'm trying to come up with ways to save Majestic."

"Uh-huh. Let's see what you've got there." Lillian reached across the table to pull the pad out of her grip. " 'Sell the car.' Oh, sweetie, that's not such a good idea."

"Why not? The Spyder's fully paid for. It's only four years old and in excellent condition. At least that'll help defray the costs for the Bardonellis' access ramp. If we could hold on for another few weeks, maybe we can pull out of this slump."

"And leave you dependent on public transportation to get to work? I don't like the idea of you taking the subway at night. Besides, how much will you pay to travel from Queens to that nursing home every week? Trains and buses would never get you there, and a taxi would cost you a small fortune. Trust me." She tapped the article again. "This is your best bet."

"What about Nana?"

Lillian waved a dismissive hand in the air. "I'll keep an eye on Nana. Leave me the keys to your car, and I'll drive out there every Thursday just as you do."

"Can you drive?"

"Well, it's been a while, but somehow I don't think automobiles have changed that much since 1956."

"Actually, Lillian, they've changed a lot."

"Then I'll have Marcus drive."

Marcus, their building's fifty-something maintenance man, nearly tripped over himself every time he saw the willowy septuagenarian. Lillian might have retired from the Rockettes twenty-five years ago, but she still fought to maintain what she called her "girlish figure," with very satisfactory and unusual results.

Clearly, Lillian wasn't about to take no for an answer, but Renata couldn't pick up and run off to participate in some game show. She had responsibilities here. Buzzing with Lillian's well-meaning but misguided advice, she reread the *Times* article, seeking another avenue of escape.

"It says here the show is for newlyweds."

"So, get married."

"Just like that?" she said, snapping her fingers.

"Just like that. Surely you know a man who'd marry you for the chance to win a million dollars. What about your partner?"

"Connell?" She shook her head. "Forget it."

"Why? Is he married?"

"No."

"He said he'd agree to anything you came up with, didn't he?"

"Yes, but—"

"Is it his looks? Does he resemble Quasimodo? Because let me tell you, Kissinger was no prince in the looks department either, but that man had a way of making a woman feel like a queen . . ." Her eyes grew dreamy. "Oh, yes, that man was one in a million. His politics might have been questionable—"

"Enough, Lillian. I don't have the strength to discuss Cambodia and the Nixon years right now."

Lillian's eyes reverted to black and probing. "So you'll do it? You'll ask this Connell fellow to go along with you?"

She shrugged in surrender. "I'll ask him."

What was the worst that could happen?

Connell slammed his palm over the newspaper article, pushing it across the desktop. "A reality game show? How about we run off to Atlantic City and hit the casinos? We'd have better odds."

"But don't you see? This," Renata tapped a finger atop the black type, "is our chance to get out from under."

Leaning back in the soft leather chair, he stared at the speckled dots in the ceiling tiles. He silently counted to ten at least three times, but resentment rose in his throat like smoke up a chimney. When she'd called an hour ago and asked to see him, he thought she had a real solution for their problems. Instead, she showed up peddling a pipe dream.

"First of all, we're not newlyweds; we're not even a couple."

She waved off his concern with a flick of her wrist. "A quick trip to City Hall could remedy that," she said. "Unless you have some other emotional attachment at the moment?"

Amazed at her audacity, he leaned across the metal desk and knocked on her forehead. "Is anyone in there? You're not suggesting we get married, are you?"

She pulled away from his reach with a frown. "Why not? It could be a business arrangement. Contestants must be newlyweds married less than a year. We could pretend to be a couple madly in love for a month, couldn't we? It's for a good cause."

"And what happens if we don't make it on the show?"

"We get a quickie divorce, irreconcilable differences or some such nonsense. What's the big deal? Look how many celebrities get drunk in Las Vegas, marry someone totally inappropriate, and call it quits when they sober up."

"We're not celebrities, Renata. And I'm not sure I want to become one thanks to televised exposure on some freak show."

"You've seen how these survival shows operate. For heaven's sake, you're a master carpenter, I'm a registered nurse. Between the two of us, we could handle anything they throw our way. When we win, we use part of the money to get Majestic Health Contractors back in the black. The rest, we split, fifty-fifty."

"I'll think about it. Okay?"

Sensing she might argue, he focused on the contract atop his desk, signaling an end to the meeting. Through the filter of his lashes, he watched her fold the newspaper before tucking it in her purse. The air stirred, revitalizing her exotic perfume. His nose sent silent messages to his mind, subtle invitations to envelop himself in her sweet aroma. He shook the feeling away.

Renata was off-limits, his business partner, nothing more. And she was involved with someone else. Okay, maybe not anymore, but that didn't mean he wanted to be her rebound man.

"You don't have long to think. Contestants will be chosen Monday."

Shaking his head in bewilderment, he tried to concentrate on the legal words in the paper before him. Unfortunately, the enormity of her presence in the tiny room made it impossible to focus on anything else.

Marriage? To Renata? Ridiculous!

He'd only considered marriage once in his lifetime. Annie McCutcheon, with soft blond hair and big green eyes, was completely different from the dark and exotic Renata. And Annie also had a weakness for his younger brother, Duncan.

A faded vision glimmered in the recesses of his brain, a couple locked in a passionate kiss, a gasp of surprise. . . . He shoved the image back where it could do no harm.

Now he studied the expression on Renata's face, and his heart softened. The tight clenching of her jaw, the moisture brimming in her eyes, the adorable way she tucked her lower lip behind her teeth, all evidenced how much this idea meant to her. Poor Renata had pinned her hopes of financial solvency on a game show. Only a cold-blooded monster would dash those dreams.

"All right," he relented with a deep sigh.

Her entire face glowed with joy. "Thank you! You won't regret this, I promise."

I already do, he thought.

Renata never knew what to expect when she took the two-and-a-half-hour drive to Whispering Pines Nursing Home each week. Some days, Nana's mind surrendered to senile dementia, which threatened to remove her memories permanently. Far less frequently, Nana retained her sharp edge and quick wit.

Today, Renata stood in the hall watching the fragile

lady in the green vinyl chair fuss with an embroidery hoop. Morning sunlight from a nearby window surrounded her silver head like an angel's halo. A fitting tribute.

Nana's brow furrowed as she worked a difficult stitch in her needlepoint. Whatever the problem, she solved it quickly enough, evidenced by her satisfied grin. Cataracts might have clouded the old lady's sight, but they would never dim her ability to make a barren cloth come to life with little more than a needle, a basket of colorful threads, and some patience.

Pasting on a cheerful smile, Renata rapped on the door and walked inside. The warm scent of bleach, powdery and clean, cocooned her in comfort. "Hi, Nana. How are you feeling today?"

The lady looked up and beckoned Renata closer, tilting her chin for a kiss. "Rennie, *innamorata,* is it Thursday already?"

"Sure is." After kissing Nana's chapped, leathery cheek, she sat on the edge of the bed and slapped her hands atop her lap. "So. What would you like to do today?"

"Oh, I don't know." Nana turned to look at the scenery outside. "It's a nice day. Maybe we could get sno-cones from the cafeteria then walk around the park a bit."

She studied the purplish circles under Nana's eyes. "Maybe we should stick to a walk in the garden."

"Can we still get sno-cones?"

Renata bit back a laugh at the childish plea. "Yes."

"Okay, then, the garden it is. Oh, that reminds me. Look." She unclipped the embroidery hoop and straightened the cloth to display its pattern. Hundreds of French knots and satin stitches created roses, gladioli, and cherry trees beneath yellowish streetlights lining a stone bridge. "What do you think?"

"It's lovely."

"I'm glad you like it. I made it for you and Steve. To put in your house after your wedding." She craned her neck to look out into the hallway. "He didn't come with you today?"

"Nana, Steve and I broke up."

Steve was now in the tropics, rubbing coconut oil over the golden body of his bride. If she had one more chance at him . . .

"You and Steve broke up?" Nana's question shattered her musings just when a giant condor was about to swoop down from the sky and carry Steve off Rio's white sand beach.

"Mmm-hmm."

"Thank God. I never liked him. He had cat eyes, you know."

"Cat eyes? What does that mean?"

"Watch a cat sometime, *innamorata.* Even when they look at you, they don't really see you. They look through you. Almost as if they're planning how to eat you. The only time you can trust a cat is with liverwurst. Do you remember when Grampa owned the little grocery store in Canarsie? He'd test the supplier's liverwurst by feeding it to that stray cat in the alley. If the cat didn't eat it, Grampa didn't buy it."

"I remember."

Nana lifted a bony finger to shake in the air. "Never marry a man with cat eyes. Find a man who sees you, even when he isn't looking at you. Like your Grampa. He was a good man. I loved him 'til the day he died." She leaned forward in her chair, so close Renata smelled the cologne and dusting powder on her neck, the familiar old-fashioned fragrances of lily of the valley and lavender. "Do you want to hear a secret?"

"Sure."

"Young people of today don't know what love is. They confuse lust for love. Love isn't fireworks and sunsets on the beach. That's lust. Love is simpler. It's holding hands while doing the most mundane things, like sitting on a couch watching TV. It's relying on one another through thick and thin. Love doesn't weaken a man and woman; it gives them strength to do things they didn't know possible. When you wake in the morning next to a man and have thoughts of nothing more than making love, that's lust. But when you wake in the morning with thoughts of every minute you'll spend together, that's love."

Her trembling hands folded the embroidered cloth into an even white square before tucking it into the top of her ever-present wicker sewing basket. "Only get married when you've found a man you love who loves you back. Settle for nothing less and you'll be happy all the days of your life."

Oh, Nana, if you only knew . . .

Chapter Three

Although the Marriage Bureau inside City Hall teemed with excited couples of all ages and backgrounds, the room hardly displayed an inspiring beginning to wedded bliss. Cement brick walls painted a nauseating shade of pea green didn't soothe an anxious bride's dipping stomach. Rows of shoddy wooden folding chairs clustered near gunmetal gray desks where employees hunched over mountains of paperwork, lending the proceedings an assembly-line quality.

In the first row, a pregnant teenager in a white lace maternity blouse sat beside a brooding young man sporting orange spiked hair and a black T-shirt with an airbrushed tuxedo jacket on the front. In the second row, an older couple, perhaps in their mid-fifties, whispered to each other while waiting their turn to stand before the justice of the peace. The love they shared showed in minute details—the way he leaned his head near her shoulder to murmur in her ear, the easy touch she used to brush an imaginary piece of lint from his jacket.

With her own situation so different from these others,

Renata turned away from the excited soon-to-be-wedded and paced in the narrow aisle. Unease crept down her spine on padded paws to dig sharp talons into her stomach. Her self-control teetered, but Renata clamped down the urge to run her fingers through her hair in anxiety. Lillian had spent over twenty-five minutes winding the heavy mass into a French braid interspersed with white silk rosebuds.

"Not quite as bridal as a veil," she'd said with a wink, "but it gives some indication today is a connubial event."

So did the bouquet of white and peach roses sprinkled with baby's breath Renata had, on impulse, asked a neighborhood florist to create. Now, in the closeness of the room, the roses she clutched looked much as she felt, slightly wilted and tired around the edges.

What had possessed her to propose such a scheme? And to Connell, of all people? Oh, he was good-looking, in a Paul Bunyan rugged kind of way. Curls of golden-red hair tousled over bright blue eyes. Angular cheekbones and a strong chin routinely coated with a day's growth of beard gave him a scruffy look she'd normally find irresistible.

"Renata." Connell stood in the doorway to the Marriage Bureau, huffing and puffing as if he'd run a marathon.

"Sorry I'm late, but I had to stop on Canal Street to buy this." Between his thumb and forefinger, he held a gold band.

She barely glanced at the ring, her focus more intent on the Prince Charming who displayed it. My God. In the three years she'd known Connell, he never looked more appealing than he did at this moment. Perhaps the richness of the black suit framing those mile-wide shoulders distracted her. Or maybe she'd forgotten that his eyes reflected the pure blue of a perfect June sky. Whatever.

Something about his appearance right now set her nerves floundering in a sea of confusion.

Following her gaze, he looked down at himself, then up into her face. Sweeping his arms out in a wide arc, he flashed a smug grin. "I know. I clean up pretty good, don't I? This is my wedding-slash-funeral suit. I don't get to wear it too often so it's probably overkill, but it *is* an Armani."

Using exaggerated motions, he moved like a fashion model for a men's magazine. Holding up a bent wrist to look at his watch, then segueing into the thoughtful pose of an executive extending a fingertip toward his temple, before ending the farce by tossing his head back as if mutely laughing at a joke.

Each larger-than-life stance, intended to lighten her mood, had the opposite effect. Until now, Renata had only seen him at work, in his office or atop a roof, where he wore a full day's worth of stubble on his cheeks while his mop of curly hair stayed clamped under a Yankees baseball cap or whipped around in the wind. His normal attire consisted of flannel work shirts in the winters, T-shirts in the summers, dusty jeans, and heavy black boots.

But inside City Hall, Connell the Lumberjack had disappeared, replaced by Connell the Humorous Sophisticate. With a boyish quality due to freshly shaved cheeks, he exuded enough charm to melt the hardest New York cabbie's heart.

While she continued to gape, he stopped posing and shook his head. "You've changed your mind about this, haven't you?"

"N-no," she stammered, unable to tear her eyes away from the broad expanse of shoulders enshrouded in midnight black wool. One thought ran through her mind, making her sense of logic scatter like autumn leaves in a November wind.

He looks good enough to eat!

"Thanks." He nodded at her white silk suit and smirked. "So do you."

Oh, God, had she said that aloud? Judging by the smug expression on his face and the way he smacked his lips at her, she must have. Flames of humiliation licked her cheeks and fanned out past her ears. To cover her embarrassment, she coughed and rasped out through a drying throat, "Let's say the vows and get this over with."

Rubbing his hands together in mock glee, he waggled his eyebrows. "You bet. Let's get hitched."

Completing the necessary paperwork took a total of five minutes. They then spent over an hour and a half sitting in the awful folding chairs, waiting to speak their vows.

"It's hard enough accepting the fact we're having a sham marriage," she whispered. "I can live without the romance, the church, the attendants, and the reception. But I can't help but feel as if we just filed for a bank loan."

"Nah." Connell smirked. "It takes a lot more paperwork to apply for a loan."

At long last, the clerk yelled out, "Moon and MacAllister!" And on stiff legs, she rose from the chair to walk beside Connell to where the justice of the peace waited.

In ten minutes, the ceremony ended. No fanfare, no rice, no bouquet toss. Two simple words spoken by each of them and a terse, "I now pronounce you man and wife. You may kiss the bride."

Oh, Lord, she'd forgotten about this part. Judging by Connell's gape, he hadn't considered it either. Still, he shrugged, flashed her that charming smile, and then leaned in for the kill. His callused hands caressed the sides of her cheeks as he pressed his lips to hers.

The moment they touched, their mouths fused together in a soldered steel bond. She couldn't break away from him if she tried. An undeniable heat consumed her, saturating her pores, wilting her like the forgotten flowers in her grasp. As their kiss deepened, she swayed on legs as firm as dandelion stems in a brisk wind.

"Next!" The judge's acetone voice ripped them apart, leaving her to stare at Connell in bewilderment.

Get a grip, Renata. Steve's been gone less than a week and here you are, falling for another pair of skillful lips.

"Shall we?" Connell wound her arm around his elbow.

Renata nodded, too confused to speak. How could he appear so unaffected by the heat of that kiss? Right now, her legs barely had enough strength left to support her shaking body. An uncontrollable urge flourished to grab him by those gorgeous lapels and plant a kiss on him that made his knees buckle. Somehow she resisted the temptation and managed to walk past the broken-down chairs, out of the office, and into the bright sunshine of a hot afternoon.

Traffic idled on the street outside while thousands of men and women pushed and shoved their way around the crowded sidewalks. Rush hour, a New Yorker's favorite nightmare, played in full swing around them.

"Okay," he said, checking off an imaginary list in the air. "We got married. What happens next?"

She shrugged. "Not much. Monday morning at nine A.M., we bring our marriage license to the lobby of the Summerhouse Hotel on West 65th Street. We'll find out the rest of the details when we get there."

"The Summerhouse, eh?"

She nodded.

"How'd you like to get a jump on the other contestants?"

"How?"

"I renovated the Summerhouse a few years back. I know the manager fairly well. He'll cut us a break on a room. What do you say we have a mini-honeymoon there this weekend?" He must have seen her eyes narrow in suspicion because he held up his hands in surrender. "We'll get a suite, and I'll sleep on the couch. This way, Monday morning we can be on line before all the other suckers. Whaddya think?"

"Yes," she answered without hesitation, racing down the steps, her arm upheld to hail one of the unoccupied cabs idling in the midtown traffic jam. "Definitely. Let's do it. But first, I want to go home and pack a few things."

Before she could open the door to an on-duty taxi, Connell reached around her to grasp the handle. Seated inside, she breathed a sigh of relief. Another good omen—they'd actually flagged down a cab with working air-conditioning.

Settling beside her, Connell gave the driver the address to her apartment in Queens.

"You got it," the cabbie said in a heavily accented tongue.

Once on their way, uncomfortable silence enveloped the cab, broken only by the dispatcher's staticky directions to other drivers spitting from the radio. She supposed Connell felt as strange about their situation as she. Questions flitted inside her head like the butterfly exhibit at the Bronx Zoo. What would happen now? Had she lost her mind? Could she go through with this, spending a month on some desert isle, playing Mary Ann to his Professor? Could they convince a group of strangers they were a happy newlywed couple, head over heels in love?

A funny thought popped into her head. "At least I won't have to change my monogrammed towels."

"Renata MacAllister," Connell remarked and shrugged. "I guess it could be worse."

"That's for sure. If I'd married Steve, I would've been Renata Perotta."

Connell snorted, and for the first time in days, Renata broke into a fit of endless giggles.

When she and Connell walked into her apartment a short while later, a balm of serenity soothed her frazzled nerves.

"Make yourself at home," she told him as she pulled the key from the lock and closed the door.

He took a seat at her kitchen table, and his long legs thrust out across the linoleum floor. Everything in the kitchenette, not very large to begin with, dwarfed beneath his presence. Her imagination took flight. She lived in a dollhouse, and King Kong had just stopped by for tea.

"I'm going to change then I'll make us something to eat."

Unease whispered through her at the idea of getting undressed with Connell only a few yards away. But she reminded herself she still had home-field advantage. Better than Rolaids, her cozy little kitchen spelled relief to her. Cooking always gave her a veneer of control lacking in the rest of her life.

She'd learned at the feet of the master, one of the greatest cooks of all time, Nana. These days, whether Renata prepared a simple pasta with olive oil and garlic or an elaborate five-course meal, her mind always traveled back to those Sunday afternoons in Nana's cozy kitchen in Sheepshead Bay where the tangy smell of garlic tinged the air, home-grown tomatoes ripened on a sunny windowsill, and Grampa's deep baritone crooned along to Frank Sinatra on the old stereo console in the den.

"Yoo-hoo! Rennie?" Lillian's voice called from the foyer. "Is that you? How did it go?"

Lord, the woman must have stood inside her apartment with one ear pressed to a drinking glass against the wall. Renata shook her head and slipped her shoes back on, then strode to the door to open it for her neighbor.

"Come on in, Lillian," she said, stifling the "because I couldn't stop you if I tried" part of that sentence.

"I won't disturb you long, sweetie," the old lady said. "How did everything go? Did you get—" She stopped short when Connell rose from the chair in the kitchen. "Is this him?"

Renata sighed and made the obligatory introductions. "Lillian Van Horne, this is Connell MacAllister. Lillian lives next door."

Before Renata got the last words out, Lillian sidled forward, one hand outstretched in Connell's direction. Playing the perfect gentleman, Connell lifted Lillian's hand and kissed the back of it. "I'm very pleased to meet you, Ms. Van Horne."

To Renata's intense embarrassment, Lillian actually giggled like a young girl and cooed, "Oh, please, call me Lillian." She cocked her head to the side, sending the ever-present gold turban skidding over her ear. "Now, step into the light, dear boy, so I can get a good look at you. My eyesight isn't what it used to be."

When he moved closer to her, Lillian gave him the once-over from head to toe then smiled. "Oh, Rennie. This one's a definite keeper. Tell me, Connell, has anyone ever mentioned you look like a young Gary Cooper?"

"You know, I must hear that a thousand times a day."

Lillian's cackle could crack china. "Don't tease an old lady. Now come here and give me a great big hug."

As she flung her arms wide, Renata glared at her disapprovingly. "Lillian . . ." she warned. Too late. The minute Connell stepped into the old woman's embrace, her arms enveloped him, and her hands slid down to cup his bottom. "Lillian!"

Lillian ignored her. "Yes, indeed. Just like Gary. But Gary was too skinny for my taste. You're bigger in all the right places."

Poor Connell. Even from the other side of the room, Renata saw the flood of color in his cheeks as he backed out of Lillian's hold. Still, he recovered quickly.

"You really knew Gary Cooper?"

"Knew him?" Lillian slapped him lightly across the chest. "Why, dear boy, at times he and I were quite *intimes*." In case Connell couldn't translate that little phrase, Lillian held up two fingers wrapped around one another.

Renata's eyebrows shot up in surprise. Bad enough Lillian boasted about having Henry Kissinger as a lover. Now she claimed to be intimate with Gary Cooper too? Good Lord, what famous name would pop up next? The Duke of Windsor? Hoping to stifle the groan of frustration that rose to her lips, Renata covered her lower lip behind her teeth, but the sound refused to stay within her throat and erupted with a loud hiss of air. "I'm going to change. Lillian, behave yourself while I'm gone."

"Of course, Rennie."

"What about me?" Connell asked, his smile teasing her. "Do I have to behave myself too?"

"Yes."

"Damn!" He snapped his fingers in midair. "I was hoping to find out what tempted Gary Cooper."

"Oh, you are a rascal, aren't you?" Lillian giggled again and pinched his rosy cheeks. "I'm far too old for you."

"You're only as old as you feel, Lillian."

"Well, while I was feeling you, I was twenty-one again."

Enough. Renata couldn't take any more. With a sigh, she turned and stomped down the hallway to her bedroom. After kicking off her shoes, she unwound the braid from the back of her head and removed the silk rosebuds to untie the separate strands. Once she'd brushed out the tangles, she pulled the mass off her face, clipping it with a large tortoise-shell barrette. By the time she changed into white pants and a muted floral top then padded back into the kitchen, Lillian had disappeared.

"Don't tell me you scared her off," she said to Connell as she draped a bib apron over her head.

"No, she had dinner on the stove and didn't want to set the apartment on fire. Damned decent of her, if you ask me. She said she'd come back in a little while. She has something for you."

Mmm, she could just imagine what Lillian had for her. A thousand images came to mind, each one more ridiculous than its predecessor. One of Jacqueline Kennedy's pillbox hats, a guitar broken by Jimi Hendrix at Woodstock, Nikita Khrushchev's shoe, Errol Flynn's recipe for fruitcake, the list went on and on.

Renata shook the grainy visions off the black-and-white television screen in her head. "At least we can eat in peace." Her statement met with silence, and like so many times in the past, a hurried apology flew to her lips. "I'm sorry about Lillian. She's a little much when you first meet her, but she grows on you after a while."

"Don't apologize. I like her."

"You do?" Even after two years, Steve had never understood her friendship with Lillian.

"Sure. She reminds me of Norma Desmond from that old movie. The one with Gloria Swanson? *Sunset Boulevard.* She's a crazy old bird, but fun. She told me she was a Rockette at Radio City Music Hall for thirty years. I bet she has some wild stories."

"Don't believe everything she tells you. I doubt half the amusing anecdotes she shares ever really happened to anyone, much less to her." She reached into a lower cabinet and pulled out a stockpot. "Is pasta okay with you?"

"Sounds great. Can I help?"

"Can you make a salad?"

"Only if I use one of those kits in a bag," he admitted with a guilty wince.

"Then sit back and relax," she ordered. "I'll take care of it. Besides, I wouldn't want you to get anything on that suit. I don't think my sweats will fit you."

Turning to the sink, she filled the pot with cold water, added a dash of salt, and set it on the stove-top over a high flame. She then pulled out a jar of marinara sauce, placing it on the counter while she dug for a saucepan.

"Jarred sauce?" He clucked his tongue. "I'm terribly disappointed, Renata. I thought I was getting a real Italian wife—the kind who cooked from scratch."

"You are. I jar my own sauce."

His eyes widened, and he sat up higher in the chair. "Really? I was only kidding. Don't go to so much fuss."

She waved him off. "It's our wedding night. We should make a little fuss, right?"

After pouring the sauce into the pan and setting it on the stove, she sat down in the chair across from him. She focused on his face, looking for complete honesty when she continued this conversation. "Can I ask you something?"

"Shoot."

"Have you ever cheated on a girlfriend?"

He never batted an eye, never looked away from her. "No."

"You're good," she said, pointing a finger at him. "Almost had me fooled."

"The truth of the matter is," Connell added in a softer tone, "I'd never condone cheating in a relationship."

He sounded so sincere she found it hard not to believe him. Maybe even impossible. "So then, why did Steve do it?"

"You mean, why did he cheat? How should I know what was going on in his head?"

"I don't know." The weight of the world crushed her shoulders and she slammed a palm on the table, wishing Steve's face could feel the impact. "I just—I just thought I knew him so well, you know?"

He reached across the table to cup her hand, and the crushing weight balanced a bit, leaving her lighter and stronger at the same time. "If I had known what he was planning, I would have stopped him from hurting you before it happened."

"Oh, yeah? How?"

His hand moved from hers to cup her chin. "I would have married you sooner."

A jolt of electricity shot through her, and she jumped back as if burned. "The pasta," she said to cover her reaction. "I have to add the pasta."

She moved to the stove and leaned her face over the pot of boiling water. It only served to add to her rising body temperature, but at least it gave her a reasonable explanation for the sweat beading on her forehead and the fire glowing in her cheeks.

Just remember, this is a business deal, nothing more.

Stay detached. If you don't, when this marriage comes to its inevitable conclusion, he'll take the only thing you have left—your pride. Don't let that happen. Please don't let that happen.

Chapter Four

Connell pushed his empty plate to the middle of the table. "Wow! That was the best meal I've had in ages." He bit back a laugh when Renata preened. "Maybe I should forget about this game show and stay married to you. My appetite would never forgive me if I let you go without a fight."

She must have picked up on the double entendre in his statement. That dusky blush washed over her face again, and her lashes fluttered against her high cheekbones. Glistening eyes stared at him in surprise, drowning his gaze in warm honey. He could taste the sweetness on his tongue; it reminded him of the moment he'd kissed her inside City Hall. She'd make one hell of a dessert right now.

In an attempt to keep from lunging across the table, he sat on his hands and pictured Chelsea Bardonelli stuck in her parents' den because she couldn't maneuver her wheelchair up the stairs to her bedroom. Not even that image cooled his blood. Only one thing that kept him from crushing her to him. One thing squelched the itch to dance his fingers through her hair, to caress the curve of her jaw, to taste her lips. Only fear of her reaction kept him from indulging his fantasy.

Bang, bang, bang! Saved by the knock. Better than fear, the intrusion worked like a bucket of ice water to douse the fire.

"That's probably Lillian again," Renata said, rising. "You want to get the door while I clear the table?"

He shrugged. "No problem."

Yeah, sure. No problem. With halting steps, he walked to the door, opened it, and saw no one. Then a screech pierced his ears, and his gaze traveled downward. He blinked twice, looked up at the ceiling, then down again, but the view didn't change. Beneath a scrap of white gauze lay a pair of feathered cheeks with what looked like circles of heavy orange rouge.

"Um, Renata," he called over his shoulder. "I know we didn't have wine with dinner, and you're probably not going to believe this, but there's a bird in a bridal veil out here."

Her laughter sent butterflies flitting across the base of his back. "That's Buttons. Lillian's probably on her way."

"The woman has a pet parrot?"

Lillian's responsive cackle sounded like the scratch of an old phonograph needle. "She's a cockatiel, Connell. A gift from an admirer many years ago. And speaking of gifts . . ." She appeared in the hallway holding a large box wrapped in white paper with a giant silver bow.

"Here," he offered. "Let me take that from you."

"Thank you." As she passed the parcel, she poked a bony elbow into his ribs. "Actually," she continued in a raspy whisper indicative of someone who had smoked heavily at one time, "the original Buttons died in 1968. This is Buttons III."

With her signature whistle, Buttons hopped inside and sat on the back of the sofa.

"You must really love cockatiels," he said, staring in fascination at the creature peeking at him through the gauzy white veil.

Lillian shook her head. "I loved Oscar."

"Oscar?"

"Oscar Hammerstein. We worked together in the original Broadway production of *South Pacific*. I was a chorus girl then. He gave me my first Buttons as a token of his affection. When I brought her home, the owner of this building was less than enthused about having a cockatiel roaming around." She winked. "I used my powers of persuasion to gain his permission to keep her. But he insisted that once she died, no more birds. Thus, every time a Buttons dies, I replace her before the landlord finds out."

"So he and the owner think you have the world's oldest living cockatiel."

"It's the only way to keep the memory of my dear Oscar alive." While Connell closed the door, Lillian stepped into the kitchen. "Rennie? I brought you and Connell a wedding present."

Renata turned from the sink and wiped her hands on the skirt of her apron. "That really wasn't necessary, Lillian. You know the details of this wedding better than anyone."

Connell's eyes swept from the old lady to the young one. "She does?"

"Ha!" Lillian retorted. "Who do you think came up with the idea for you two to elope and try out for that game show?"

"You mean Renata didn't dream this up on her own?" he asked, placing the white box in the center of the table.

"Safe, responsible, play-by-the-rules Renata? Ha!"

Safe, responsible, play-by-the-rules Renata? He'd yet to meet that woman. He only knew Renata the Risk Taker, a woman more than capable of dreaming up a quickie wedding followed by a stint on a game show.

"So," Lillian prompted. "What do you plan to do between now and Monday? Are you two going to stay here? You can't live apart or the television people might find out and become suspicious."

"We already thought of that," Renata replied. "Connell plans to get us a suite at the Summerhouse for the weekend."

Another sharp jab in the ribs brought him back into the discussion. "Smart man," Lillian murmured. "That'll give you an edge over the competitors come Monday morning."

He took a step out of her elbow's range before nodding his agreement. "I sure hope so. We'll go our separate ways for work, but at all other times we'll remain inside the suite."

"Then what are you doing here?"

"I had to change before heading to the hospital," Renata said. "Just because I got married doesn't mean I can afford to skip work." She turned to Connell. "We should go. I'll get my bag."

"Wait," Lillian said. "You haven't opened your gift yet."

"Lillian, this is not exactly a gift-giving occasion."

"Of course it is. You got married, silly! Now open it."

He peered over her shoulder as she slowly unwrapped one corner then another then turned the box over to loosen the tape along the bottom. Morbid curiosity finally got the better of him. "Will you open it already?"

"I'm opening it. Just give me a minute if you don't mind."

"It's wrapping paper, for God's sake, not a bandage. Just rip it off."

"It's pretty wrapping paper, and I want to save it."

At long last, the paper fell from the box, and Connell said a silent prayer heavenward that the box wasn't taped also. Apparently someone upstairs heard his plea. The lid rose without a hitch.

He looked down again and came face-to-face with a riot of colors. Vivid red, green, blue, yellow, and purple splashed into his eyes with the force of a cartoon coming to life. A familiar face, minus the turban, floated in the center of this stormy sea of hues, looking pathetically lost among the waves with little rhyme or reason.

"It's a portrait of me," Lillian said with pride. "Painted many years ago by a starving art student in the Village."

"It's . . . lovely," Renata replied.

"Oh, I'm so glad you like it! Andrew always said I had a face indicative of the classical Greeks. And I wanted to give you something from the heart, but I didn't have enough time to shop the way I would have liked. Who knows? In another twenty years, this might be worth something."

Renata hugged the old woman. "It wasn't necessary to give us a gift at all. But thank you just the same. It's so unusual and very . . ." she hesitated for a brief moment, ". . . you."

Lillian stepped close to Connell to embrace him. Recalling their last encounter, he moved a kitchen chair between them. "You shouldn't have." He leaned over the obstacle and wrapped his arms around her bony shoulders. "It's more than we ever anticipated."

"Bah!" A wave of ringed fingers flew before his face, but Lillian's gaze remained directed at Renata. "You'd better give me your car keys."

Renata's face paled. "Why don't we wait to see if that's necessary first. After all, I could be back here first thing Monday morning."

"Trust me." Lillian shook her head. "I have a sense about these things. You won't be back until you've won the million. Now do you want me to watch over Nana or not?"

Connell's curiosity piqued. "Nana?"

"Yes, Nana's her—"

"My cat," Renata interjected.

"Really? I didn't know you had a cat."

"Mmm-hmm," Lillian said with a cackle he couldn't fathom. "Had her for years now. An Italian shorthair."

"I've never heard of that breed. What does she look like?"

"She's a rare creature, that Nana. Pretty little thing, gray and white with big brown eyes like Renata's."

He looked around the apartment, but only saw Buttons on the back of the couch in her white dress and veil. "Is it safe for the bird to be loose with a cat on the prowl? Or is Nana locked up?"

"She's at the vet's." Renata's gaze never left the table.

"I'm sorry. I hope it's not serious."

Renata frowned. "Unfortunately, it is."

Her voice took on a hard undertone, and he had an overwhelming urge to pull her into his arms. To comfort and assure her. He took a step forward.

"We should go." She grabbed Lillian's elbow and steered her to the door. "Thanks for stopping by, Lillian, and for the gift."

"You're welcome, sweetheart," Lillian replied, confusion clouding her wrinkled brow. "Buttons, come along. Let's leave these two to get better acquainted."

From the living room, Connell watched Lillian pull Renata into a tight embrace. The old lady whispered in her ear, but he was too far away to hear. Whatever she said didn't sit well with Renata. Her lips disappeared in a tight line as she shook her head emphatically. But when Lillian and Buttons were out of sight and she faced him again, the grim expression had disappeared.

"What was that all about?" he asked.

"What? Oh, Lillian? Nothing. She keeps jumping into things when she doesn't have all the facts."

I know it's none of my business, Renata, but I think if you learned to trust Connell, he could make you very happy . . .

Lillian's words echoed in Renata's head like a battle hymn. No. She shook her head emphatically, just as she had when Lillian first uttered the ridiculous advice. No, no, no. A thousand times no. She couldn't trust anyone, not with Nana's personal problems. She and Connell had agreed to a business arrangement, nothing more. It wouldn't be fair to saddle him with the true extent of her financial woes.

From what she'd seen of Connell over the last few years, he was a guy with a heart. Look how quickly he'd agreed to this crazy game show idea. For her. Because she'd asked—no, *begged*—him to do it. Unlike Steve, who'd run off with someone else, if Connell knew about Nana and the nursing home bills, he might feel obligated to stay married to her out of pity. She shivered at the thought.

No. She had to keep her secret, maintain as much distance from her husband as possible, and free him from their sham marriage as soon as the game show stint ended, whether that day came tomorrow or next month.

Mind made up, she followed Connell out of his apartment and across the street to the underground parking garage.

"You work at St. John of Parma, right?" He clicked a

button on the keypad dangling from his hand. In response, a pickup truck's headlights blinked twice in rhythm with the bip-beep of the disengaging alarm and click-clack of the door locks.

"Yes, why?"

"I'll drop you off before going to the Summerhouse." He opened the passenger door then lifted their suitcases to place them behind the seat.

"No, that's okay," she replied, taking a step toward the street. "I'll just take the train."

"No way, Renata, I'm not going to allow you to ride the train at this time of night."

Pique punched her brain with puckered fists. "Did you just say you won't 'allow' me?"

"I'm sorry. Poor choice of words."

"You better believe it! Just because you and I are married doesn't mean you own me, Connell. Until Monday, I'm going to continue my life as I always have."

Even under the dim overhead lights of the parking garage, she saw his eyebrows shoot up in surprise. "Oh? And you always take a train and a subway to work? Alone?"

"Well, no, I usually drive."

"Do you even know where you are right now?"

"No." She hated to admit that, and he probably knew it.

Settling a hand on her arm, he drew her toward the truck's interior. "Just get in. Please?"

Temper flaring, she yanked her arm out of his grasp. He was right. She knew it, even before she slid into the truck and stared out the windshield at the cement walls. What was wrong with her? She should be grateful for his thoughtfulness. The idea of standing all alone on a subway platform in a strange place in the middle of the night sent icy shivers down her spine that the city's heat and humidity couldn't reach. But the idea of spending time in Connell's close company terrified her more.

Only married a few hours and he already made it too easy to rely on him. And she knew better than to count on anyone but herself. Not after what Steve did. She couldn't afford to fall for compliments and kindhearted gestures again.

Why, the week before he left, Steve brought a dozen red roses home with a card that read, "Just because. . . ." In hindsight, he probably got them to appease his guilty conscience. At the time, though, she'd thought it an indication that he loved her wholly. When she'd gone to work that night, she'd actually boasted to two of the other triage nurses that he'd pop the question any day now. And by God, he had.

Just not to her.

Her head slumped. With her scars still open and bleeding, she'd be a fool to trust another man. And Renata Jacqueline Moon MacAllister might be many things, but not a fool. She could think of only one way around this impasse. She'd have to play the Spoiled Princess role. She hated the idea, but the alternative, declaring peace and in a weak moment, possibly falling for him, terrified her more.

"I'm sorry if I sound like an overbearing ass." He slid into the driver's seat and started the truck's engine. "But we have no idea what's going to happen with this game show. We don't even know how they'll choose contestants on Monday. Until then, it's important we look like a happy newlywed couple."

"Why don't you let me handle the details?" she snapped. "I have it all worked out. You worry about holding up your end of the deal, and I'll worry about the rest."

He sighed. "Tell me, Renata, is there a particular reason you insist upon characterizing me as a bad guy? Because as far as I know, *I'm* the one man who agreed to your cockamamie scheme. I'm also the only contractor who agreed to donate his time and money to getting your organization off the ground."

"In the first place, Connell, this is all part of the same business deal, okay? And in the second place, anytime you want to back out, say the word and we'll back out."

With a mournful expression, he shook his head. "You're going to screw this up for us."

Better to screw up our marriage than to screw up the rest of my life, her mind screamed. But she bit her tongue and said nothing as the truck drove into the heart of the city.

Chapter Five

"Listen up, please!"

Through bleary eyes, Connell watched a bird-like woman with a beaked nose and pouffy hair stuffed beneath a safari hat attempt to gain control of the room. Between her pecking actions and her khaki shorts and top, she resembled Mick Jagger's rendition of a sparrow.

Nothing quieted the horde of impassioned newlyweds clamoring in the Summerhouse lobby at nine o'clock Monday morning. Hundreds of couples, ranging in age from early twenties to mid-sixties, crowded into the open room until the revolving doors could no longer turn due to the press of bodies inside.

Meanwhile, the dangling bullhorn banged against her chest, and the sound reverberated with a rhythmic thunk through the amplifier she'd left on. When her chaotic movements didn't do enough to silence the crowd, she lifted the horn to her mouth.

"Ladies and gentlemen, if I might have your attention, we can go over what will occur this morning. People, please!"

The ear-splitting screech of feedback as the bullhorn came into proximity with the microphone silenced everyone. The noise shot straight through Connell's ears into his brain.

"Sorry," Birdie mumbled before pulling the bullhorn up over her head and handing it to a nearby assistant. With a wide sweep of her arms, she announced, "Ladies and gentlemen, on behalf of the Maximus Production Company, welcome to tryouts for 'The Bonds of Matri-money.' First, let me explain what you can expect. There are no contests, no games of chance. We'll simply choose five couples from today's applicants based on our own individual screening process . . ."

"What do you think?" Renata leaned close to whisper.

He raised a hand to shield his mouth from possible eavesdroppers. "I think I've seen fewer people in Times Square on New Year's Eve. How on earth are we going to stand out over so many other couples?"

"I wondered the same thing myself."

He cocked an eyebrow in her direction. "Oh, *now* you're wondering about that? What happened to the plan? I thought you had this all figured out."

Her face flooded with a furious expression, and he wouldn't have been surprised to see lightning shoot from her eyes. "Work *with* me, Connell, not against me."

Fermented sleeplessness and bitter resentment mingled to form a noxious cocktail in his belly. Like Mount Vesuvius, he stood ready to spew the boiling mixture all over his dear wife. Somehow he found the fortitude to swallow the acid, ignoring its scorching burn in his throat.

The last few days had provided him a long list of reasons why married people rarely smiled. Frustrated, irritable, self-righteous, immature, demanding, narcissistic. He'd seen every one of those qualities emerge in Renata's repertoire of emotions since Friday afternoon. Half a million dollars wasn't worth living with this much aggravation for a whole month.

"Terrific. I've pinned my future on television's answer to the Irish Sweepstakes. What do you suppose the odds are in this horserace? A million to one? Good God, how did I let you talk me into something so crazy?"

They didn't stand a snowball's chance in hell of being chosen. Even worse, he'd tied himself in matrimony to a woman who made Genghis Khan look like a pussycat. Every hope he'd harbored about this ridiculous scheme of hers collapsed under the weight of the other potential contestants pressing against him. A million smells—unpleasant body odors, sickly perfumes and aftershaves, and some kind of rice and bean combination—melded into a noxious cloud. The venomous acid roiling in his stomach gurgled loud enough to distract several nearby people from Birdie's prepared speech.

A blond woman with a face like an afghan hound gasped in outrage and stared at him over her long nose. He ignored her, but didn't miss her mumbled, "Pig."

At the insult, Renata's attention swerved to the woman with the disgusted moue on her crimson lips. She knew she was the main cause of Connell's gastrointestinal distress, but annoyance at this stranger's reaction overrode her shame.

"Did you say something?" Renata's eyes glared daggers. A frightened doe look filled the woman's features and, with a harrumph of indignation, she turned her focus back to the emcee on the stage. "I didn't think so."

She then faced her husband and saw resignation etched in his brow. Clenching her fists prevented her from pounding on his chest and weeping in frustration. How could he believe she was really this much of a witch? And how much longer would she have to play the role? God, she hated herself more every single day. She was lucky he hadn't walked out on her yet, and she wondered where he got the fortitude. Most men would have given up long ago rather than put up with the shrew she'd become. But she couldn't turn back. She'd made her bed. To that end, she forged ahead, slicing into him with a tongue sharper than a double-edged razor.

"May I remind you, my future's at stake in this also? If you have a better idea, *sweetheart,*" she stressed the endearment with silken sarcasm, "I'm all ears." He glowered at her, but said nothing. "I thought not."

The look that came into his eyes made her want to sink to the ground and beg his forgiveness. A mixture of pity, revulsion, and exhausted patience glimmered at her through their watery blue depths. And she hated herself even more for not giving in to her weakness.

One hundred yards away, behind the locked door of a hotel conference room, a closed circuit television camera scanned the throngs in the lobby. Suddenly, a finger popped down on a white button, freezing the camera's scan and sending the zoom lens to focus in on a bickering couple.

The inhabitants of the room watched a dark-haired woman, fire flashing in her eyes, castigate another woman with long blond hair and an angular face. Gaining the upper hand in that argument, she turned to a red-haired man who stood visibly complaining about something.

"She's got presence," a booming voice said with decisiveness. "I want those two."

A young bespectacled assistant turned to the head of the table, her face registering disbelief. "Those two? Mr. Oliver, are you sure?"

"Hell, yes," Mr. Oliver replied. "Just look at their faces. Look at the passion spewing from them. Viewers will love them. Ladies, young and old, will think the guy's a hunk. And there isn't a red-blooded male in America who won't be panting over her, especially after we stick her in the Bonds costume. Within two weeks, those two will double our advertising budget. I bet more than half our audience will root for that couple to win the cash. They'll be the most talked-about subject around water coolers every Monday morning. Ratings, m'girl. That's what we're after and that's what those two can provide. In spades. Get 'em. Now."

"Yes, sir." Crooking a finger, the assistant signaled to a tall man waiting patiently in the corner. Around his neck dangled a headset. At her gesture, the man slid the headphones over his hair and set a small microphone near his mouth.

"Got 'em," he said, opening the door and striding out into the throngs.

"That makes five," the assistant announced, closing her notebook with finality.

Mr. Oliver slapped his hands on the glossy tabletop and rose from his chair. "Excellent! Once we've shared the good news with our lucky couples, we'll need to verify their information. Make certain their passports and immunizations are in order. Seven days from now, they're on their way to Bali."

For Connell, the overnight flight to Bali was as comfortable as traveling in a leaky bucket attached to flying monkeys. In the window seat, ears plugged in to her Etta James collection on a handheld CD player, Renata kept her gaze transfixed on the clouds outside, saying nothing.

Squirming to find an inch of space between his knees

and the reclined seat in front of him, Connell resisted the urge to buzz the stewardess for another Bloody Mary. No way would he allow Renata's attitude make him into a boozer. No matter how difficult she made things.

The more time he spent in her miserable company, the more he regretted going along with this scheme. He'd made a lot of sacrifices to be here, but she didn't appreciate any of them.

Like taking the time off work. For her, a phone call to the personnel administrator at St. John of Parma Hospital, a subtle reminder she was entitled to three weeks' vacation and an extra week due to her recent marriage, and wham—done deal.

Connell, on the other hand, had a dilemma on his hands. He couldn't afford to close shop for at least five weeks, leaving projects unfinished and employees out of work. So, after a whole lot of soul-searching, he called his parents and asked them to come to New York and watch over things until he returned. He'd explained his sudden departure by confessing that he and Renata would be on their honeymoon. His mother screeched her joy through the phone lines. Thank God, her eldest son had finally settled down with "a nice girl." Drummond MacAllister exuded a similar excitement, though he cared more about the chance to live among the working class after five years of the dearth of retirement in Miami.

Pleasing Renata should have been so easy. What had happened to the impetuous woman who proposed an outrageous plan, sending them to City Hall for a quickie marriage, then on a flight halfway around the world? Somewhere in the last week, aliens had abducted the clever, complacent Renata and replaced her with an evil twin. As near as he could tell, the impasse started when Lillian left Renata's apartment after dinner on their wedding night. But whenever it started, his wife's icy façade continued through the rest of the week.

For seven loooong days, they remained at the Summerhouse Hotel, a DO NOT DISTURB sign dangling from their doorknob to suggest they were two newlyweds who couldn't keep their hands off each other. In reality, he slept alone in the king-sized bed all night while she worked; she, sleeping all day while he worked. When necessity forced them together physically, rancor and sarcasm kept them apart emotionally.

Narrowing his eyes, he stared at the back of her head over the top of his in-flight magazine. A mystery the plane even managed to get off the ground with the extra weight of that chip on her shoulder. So why did he find himself still drawn to her?

Crisp static from the intercom interrupted his thoughts. "Ladies and gentleman, we are about to begin our descent to Ngura Rai International Airport. Please note the captain has turned on the 'Fasten Seatbelts' sign. All trays and chairs should be in the upright position. Thank you for flying Paradise Airlines, and enjoy your stay in beautiful Bali."

As the intercom clicked off, Renata turned to glare at him. "Let's get this masquerade going," she muttered, reaching to clasp his hand. "And for God's sake, Connell, plaster a smile on your face."

Flashing a smile with no warmth, he lifted her hand to his lips, kissed the gold band on her ring finger. "Your wish is my command."

But inside the recesses of his mind, logic chastised him.

How could they possibly fool people into believing they were newlyweds if they couldn't even maintain a civil attitude toward one another? Cooperation would serve their interests better than confrontation. Hopefully, she'd realize that soon. In the meantime, he'd do everything in his power to make this work. When the time came for them to divorce, he wanted no rancor or bitterness between them. After all, they'd still be working together. At least, he hoped so. He refused to consider the idea that their marriage might destroy their business partnership.

The plane dipped lower, and the top fronds of palm trees appeared through the window. When the aircraft bumped onto the landing strip, a murmur of excitement ran through the cabin. Nineteen enthusiastic couples unbuckled their seatbelts and rose to line up in the narrow aisle.

Renata and Connell remained seated, hands gripped together as they glared at each other. Her stare only broke when a loud hiss erupted from the front of the cabin. The stewardess opened the air-locked door, and a crushing heat flew inside, wilting everything in its path, including Renata.

"God!" Releasing her clasp on Connell, she fanned herself with the back of her hand. "Do you think it's always this hot here?"

When she looked into his face again, a slow fire bubbled up from her waist to her cheeks. He stared at her as an artist might stare at the Mona Lisa, with wonder that anything so sublime could exist in the real world.

As her heart slinked up her throat, she leaned forward in the cramped seat, ignoring the armrest that dug into her abdomen. Her gaze focused on his lips, full and glistening, parted as if welcoming her to their domain.

"Well, c'mon you two," a voice with a distinctive Midwestern twang called.

"Huh?" She glanced up from Connell's mouth to see a heavy-set black woman with an orange sunbonnet flopping over her face.

The woman pointed to the bright yellow nametag pinned to Connell's chest then tapped her own. "Ain't you excited to start the game?" She waved a hand in the narrow niche of the aisle. "You can cut in front of Gilly and me if you want."

"That's so nice of you," Connell drawled as he rose and stretched lazily. "I'm Connell MacAllister and this is my wife, Renata."

"Ain't that the name of a car?" the woman asked, shaking her head in confusion.

"Not Granada, Clarice," a burly man behind her said. "Ramada. Like them fancy motels out on the interstate."

Rising to her feet, Renata stifled a groan of impatience. She'd heard every mispronunciation of her name at least a thousand times. No one ever caught it on the first fly. "Granada is a car, Ramada is a motel. But *Renata*," she emphasized each consonant, "is a woman."

"And a magnificent woman at that," Connell added, slipping an arm around her waist.

The flame banked in her cheeks flared up again.

"Oh, he's a smooth one," Mrs. Floppy-hat interjected. "No wonder you two are throwing off enough sparks to set this plane on fire. I'd keep my eyes glued on him too if he was mine."

"So, what am I, yesterday's news?" the burly man retorted.

"Of course not, Gilly-boy." She stroked a coffee-colored hand over his chest. "You know you're the only man for me."

"Hmmmph! That's better." Extending a beefy paw, he grasped Connell's hand to shake. "I'm Gilly Tompkins and this here's my wife, Clarice. We're from Iowa."

"Pleased to meet you," Connell said.

They moved in fits and starts while cheerful stewardesses at the exit thanked each debarking traveler for flying Paradise Airlines. Staring at the back of Connell's head, familiar bubbles of nervousness rumbled in Renata's stomach. Maybe she should apologize to him and ask if they might start over. The coming weeks would be easier to bear if they weren't at each other's throats.

As if sensing her thoughts, Connell leaned back slightly to whisper in her ear. "Truce?"

God, yes!

Still, she kept her tone as emotionless as possible, refusing to give an inch. "Mmm-hmm."

At last she passed through the stewardess gamut, throwing a terse nod in their direction when they wished her a pleasant stay. She stepped onto the staircase leading down to the runway, and the heat overwhelmed her. It rose from the tar in blurry opaque waves, mixed with the heavy odor of jet fuel and a lighter fragrance of exotic flowers, stinging her eyes, nose, and throat. She might have tumbled down the stairs if Connell hadn't grasped her elbow.

"You okay?"

Her mouth scorched, she nodded and concentrated on reaching the tarmac. The tinny music of metallic drums played by a group of men in teal-colored tunics and knee-length pants provided her with a rhythm for her feet to follow as she made her descent. At the bottom of the staircase, two ladies in golden dresses, wrapped sari-style around their petite frames, approached the passengers to drape them with flowered leis. When she and Connell reached the landing, they bent to accommodate the ladies' short-arms.

Distracted by the garlands of colorful blooms, she didn't notice the gentleman who slipped up behind her until he pulled her wrists behind her back. "Hey! What the—"

The sudden coolness of steel encircled her hand before she heard a noisy click. Looking down, she discovered her right wrist handcuffed to Connell's left!

"Welcome to 'The Bonds of Matri-money,'" the gentleman announced as he hustled over to the next nametag-wearing couple, a new pair of handcuffs dangling from his grip.

Chapter Six

Handcuffs!

"Perfect," Connell exclaimed. "This is beautiful. Who came up with this idea, the Marquis de Sade?"

Before Renata could reply, Clarice and Gilly, equally constrained, wandered over, eyes glazed in confusion. "Don't this beat all?" Gilly demanded, raising their handcuffed wrists into the air. "What do you think they're gonna do to us next? Put us in prison cells?"

"No," a new voice interjected. "Tents."

Renata whirled, nearly yanking Connell's arm out of its socket, to see the woman from the hotel lobby. She still wore her safari hat and khaki outfit, but binoculars replaced the bullhorn hanging from her neck.

"Did you say tents?" Clarice asked hesitantly.

"Mmm-hmm. But first, you're all going to board that bus over there." She pointed to a dilapidated old school bus wearing what looked to be a fresh coat of yellow paint and a long banner proclaiming the title, "The Bonds of Matri-money."

Renata raised her left hand and held it in front of the woman's face. "Where exactly are we going?"

"You'll learn everything you need to know en route," the woman replied.

"En route to where?" she persisted.

But the Queen of Banana Republic shooed them off as if they were recalcitrant children. "All information will be given on an 'as needed' basis. Now, get on the bus." With that, Her Majesty walked off in the direction of another group of contestants wandering around the tarmac with the very same dumbfounded expression on their faces.

"I'll show her what's needed . . ." Renata mumbled as she took a step forward, but Connell pulled her back with one quick yank on the handcuffs.

"Easy, tiger! She's not worth a million dollars. Let's just do what she says."

Grumbling to herself, she allowed Connell to lead her to the bus. Clarice and Gilly followed, and they clambered up the steps in sideways pairs like animals boarding Noah's Ark.

They found a seat ten rows back and made themselves as comfortable as possible, resting their linked hands on the scrap of duct-taped vinyl between them. While they waited, a few more couples staggered aboard, until all twenty couples sat on the bus.

After a few minutes inside the enclosed space, the air became stifling, and the heat made its moist impression on her upper lip and brow. Soft grousing began somewhere in the rear and, like a tidal wave, moved forward, increasing in volume as it traveled.

At last, a blandly handsome man dressed in the same khaki safari gear as his female counterpart boarded the bus. "Good afternoon, ladies and gentlemen. I'm Bart Meadows, the host of 'The Bonds of Matri-money.' On behalf of all the people behind the scenes, welcome to Bali."

Squirming to remove her thighs from the clammy suction of the seat, Renata turned to find a sea of impatient faces staring at Bart Meadows with pure hatred in their eyes. Amused, she gave Connell a nudge and a head jerk.

His gaze swept over the passengers. "Looks like old Bart's gonna have to win over this busload of hostile honeymooners."

"I suppose you're all wondering what you're doing here," Bart continued. A growl of agreement came from the restless. "Well, it's very simple. You all signed on to be contestants in our game show. Let me explain the rules to you."

As he reached to close the doors, he gave the driver a thumbs-up sign. The engine started with a loud belch of smelly old exhaust and a puff of black smoke. While the bus lurched forward, grinding its gears, Bart held on to the pole to keep from tumbling onto the contestants seated in the first row.

"Our first stop is the Summerhouse Hotel in Kuta," he shouted above the din. "Your luggage will be stored there while you participate in the game. Maximus Productions will provide you husbands with backpacks filled with everything you'll need for the next four weeks. We'll also release your handcuffs."

An audible sigh erupted in the bus, and Bart held up a hand for silence.

"Only long enough to change your garments in the cabanas allocated for this purpose," he announced. "Once you're re-outfitted and each husband has received a backpack, we'll snap the handcuffs on again. So long as you are active contestants in 'The Bonds of Matri-money,' the bonds must remain on. You're all newlyweds. We know you can't keep your hands off one another."

When he waggled his eyebrows for a Groucho effect, Renata sank lower in her seat, empathizing with the embarrassment he was too mindless to feel.

"Each and every task is designed for you to perform as a team. And just imagine the hijinks you'll encounter while sleeping together in handcuffs."

What? What did he say? Panic covered Renata like a sodden blanket. What kind of sadomasochistic shenanigans had she signed up for? She couldn't do this. No way. How could she possibly sleep with Connell handcuffed to her side?

"We'll figure something out," he whispered. "I promise. Just remember we're supposed to be newlyweds. We should see this as fun. Smile and pretend you're looking forward to it."

Swallowing her heart before it jumped out of her throat, she nodded. Right now, she had no choice. As if sensing her misgivings, he gave her hand a quick squeeze. His simple gesture reassured her, and she turned her attention back to Bart Meadows in time to see his trademark cheesy grin.

"The only exception to the handcuff rule will be for outhouse breaks. Let's face it, some things are too intimate to be shared, even with a spouse. At all other times, day and night, you will remain joined to your mate. When we reach camp, we'll assign you a simple challenge. Those who succeed at the task will remain as contestants and form teams. From that point on, teams will compete against one another on a daily basis.

"Those who do not succeed will immediately return to this bus. As of this moment, if you are disqualified from play, whether because your team lost a challenge or because you've given up of your own accord, you will be transported back to the Summerhouse Hotel. You will then remain in a suite at the Summerhouse, or Home Base as we call it, until the game is over and a winner has been chosen."

"So how exactly will a winner be chosen?" Gilly called from behind her.

"When only three couples remain, all of the losing couples will vote for one winning couple. That couple will receive one million dollars. The rest of you will go home with no money, but plenty of stories to tell your friends and families."

"So it becomes nothing more than a popularity contest?" Gilly complained.

"No, not really. Our challenges have been especially designed to test your marriage on as many levels as possible." Bart lifted his hands above his head and counted on his fingers. "One, camaraderie. Two, reliability. Three, stick-to-it-iveness. Four, compassion. Five . . ."

Renata leaned toward Connell. "Do you think he's using those fingers to demonstrate to us or because he can't count without 'em?"

Connell snorted back a laugh in reply.

"And last but not least," Bart said with the typical forced emphasis of a bad actor, "whichever couple is the most in love with each other."

The sly smirk on Renata's face evaporated. "We're doomed."

The Summerhouse Hotel in Kuta sat on a wide strip of white sand overlooking turquoise water. Outside the hotel, expressive faced monkeys eeked as they swung from the spiny green branches of acacia trees, bouncing tiny clusters of yellow flowers like tennis balls on a grass court. Dozens of species of birds, plumage more colorful than an ice cream shop, soared across the bright blue sky.

Their presence reminded Renata of Buttons, and a wave of homesickness washed over her.

Did Nana realize Renata was gone? She'd told Lillian to simply say she was on vacation, if Nana asked. Had Lillian visited Nana yet? Would Nana recognize Lillian? They'd been introduced several times in the past, but hadn't seen each other in over a year.

The bus lurched to a stop, shaking her back to the present.

"Ready?" Connell asked.

She nodded, and they rose to move into the aisle and out of the bus. As she stepped from the bus with Connell by her side, a loud squawk rent the sweet-smelling air. A large brown eagle swooped down from the azure sky to land in the softer, fern-like fronds and orange-red blooms of a nearby flame tree. Incredible colors and fragrances abounded in this place of smiles and sunshine. So unlike New York with its grime, smog, and crowds of grouchy people rushing about.

"It's almost magical, isn't it?" she murmured.

"Very different from home, I'll give you that."

On the busy thoroughfare, a pair of men on mopeds whizzed by, carrying overlarge pieces of wood furniture atop their shoulders. Close behind, a string of elderly ladies rode bicycles while balancing crates of eggs piled high on their silver heads.

"Did you see that? Look at those ladies. They must be carrying a thousand eggs on their heads!"

"Imagine the size of the omelet," he remarked.

"Come along, everyone!" The Queen of Banana Republic had returned, clapping her hands in a staccato rhythm while ushering the contestants from the bus to the hotel.

The hotel's exterior resembled little more than a native hut with a triangular straw roof and red-painted circular walls. But the simple façade hid a palatial interior of muted lighting, brass and glass accoutrements, plush Turkish carpets, and floral-scented air. Inside the lobby, boisterous teenagers adorned with spiky, multicolored haircuts, golden tans, kaleidoscopic swimsuits, and their requisite surfboards, laughed and called to acquaintances in a dozen different languages.

"Come along, come along." Her Highness shuffled into the lobby, still clapping her hands. "Line up and we'll release you from your bonds."

That was enough incentive for Renata. Dragging Connell with her, she raced toward the front of the line and wound up second, behind Gilly and Clarice.

When all the couples had lined up, the woman strode before them like a drill sergeant speaking to his troops. "Mr. Lester will now unlock your handcuffs, one pair at a time. When you're freed from your restraints, you will remain in an orderly line, men on the right, women on the left. We'll walk through this foyer and out those double doors in the back. Outside, you'll see several cabanas. The men will head to the cabanas on the right, the women on the left. Before you enter a cabana, one of our staff members will provide you with a bright yellow shopping bag containing a complete ensemble suitable for your needs to play this game."

A tittery voice interrupted from the rear of the lobby. "How do we know the clothes will fit us?"

"You provided us with your clothing and shoe sizes in the forms you filled out during your orientation. So, ladies, I hope you didn't lie due to vanity or you'll regret it once we're in the jungle. You will proceed inside the cabana assigned to you where you will change garments, placing your own clothing inside the bag when you're finished. Is that clear to everyone?"

A chorus of, "Yes," rang out in reply and Renata thought immediately of Mrs. Stafford's kindergarten class.

"Excellent! Then let's begin."

The same gentleman who had confined them at the airport returned now to unlock their cuffs. As the restraints fell into Mr. Lester's open hand with a clank, Renata and Connell, in unison, lifted their arms to cradle their chafed wrists. They then followed Clarice and Gilly out of the lobby, down the hall, and through the back door.

Outside, the sun blared with such magnitude Renata needed both hands cupped around her face to shield her eyes. Brilliance flashed off the water of the free-form pool, bounced into the cloudless sky and echoed back into the aqua-colored ocean, lending the atmosphere an aura of blinding white light. When her vision adjusted, she discerned the cabanas, pink doors to her left, blue doors on her right.

"How quaint," she mumbled. "Pink for girls, blue for boys."

Like matching bookends, two small-statured Balinese men gestured to the couple at the head of the line, waving their bright yellow shopping bags in the air. Clarice and Gilly approached them, took their respective bags and entered through the first doors in the rows.

Within seconds, Clarice's screeches of protest reached the other contestants. "Oh, no! I'm not spending a month in the jungle in this skimpy thing."

"Skimpy?" Renata nudged an elbow into Connell's ribs. "What does she mean by skimpy?"

Before Connell could reply, the small man on the left gestured to her to accept a shopping bag.

"Go on," Connell urged, pushing her forward. "How bad could it be? Just remember what's at stake here. One million dollars."

With a hesitant nod, she took a few steps on shaky legs while her eyes tried to perceive what exactly lay hidden behind the yellow plastic. Why couldn't she have Superman's x-ray vision for just a day?

One million dollars. She stepped into the tiny changing room and closed the door. *For one million dollars, I'll wear a bikini for a month . . .*

When she plunged her hand into the shopping bag, she pulled out a halter top and khaki shorts. She peeked inside to see if she might find another shirt, a jacket—anything else to use as a cover-up. The only other items inside were a pair of cotton socks and thick-soled hiking boots. No bra buried in the bottom. Obviously, the executive staff of Maximus Productions would use any underhanded trick to grab television ratings, even the jiggle factor.

Then again, the outfit made sense. What other garment could she change without removing handcuffs? Her alternative might have been a slinky little tube top. And running around the jungle in a halter beat bouncing out of a tube top any day of the week.

Fully dressed, as it were, she shoved the door open and stepped out to find Connell waiting.

"I sure hope they've imported sunscreen by the gallon or I'm likely to resemble a hamburger patty before this is over." Switching to a heavy brogue, he added, "We Scotsmen don't handle the sun verra well, ya ken."

Compared to her outfit, his garb covered even less flesh. No shirt at all, just shorts, and the same socks and boots she had. Maybe these television executives weren't so stupid after all. No doubt Connell's appearance on this game show would make women tune in to watch in droves.

In her opinion, there was something about a man who did physical labor for a living that was too appealing to resist. There was something so natural in the fluid motions of sinew and bone accustomed to balancing on precarious rooftops or steel girders one hundred stories up. Something that balancing a billion-dollar advertising account didn't provide. There was something in the raw sculpture of arms and legs bulked up by lifting, pounding, and working with heavy materials. Something that could never be artificially manufactured in a pristine, air-conditioned gym for a man who spent hours seated behind a desk. It was something simple, yet impossible to find anywhere. Anywhere except in the perfection of the man who stood before her now, wearing little more than a boyish grin and a pair of khaki shorts.

What was wrong with her? This was Connell, for God's sake. Connell, who'd only agreed to go along with her cockamamie scheme to keep their organization from sinking into financial ruin.

Why did her mind suddenly long for those rough-hewn arms to hold her against his chiseled chest? Why did she burn to feel his fingers running up under her hair? Why did she have an incredible urge to press her lips to his, to taste his breath inside her mouth?

Familiarity. Connell was the only thing familiar to her right now. She was in a foreign country, thousands of miles from home, with a bunch of strangers. Connell represented her sole link to her old life, to Nana and Lillian and Buttons, to her comfortable apartment, and to Majestic Health Contractors. Finding Connell attractive had more to do with homesickness than romance. Steve's betrayal was too new, too painful, for her to think about another relationship. She still cringed whenever she thought about the way he broke up with her. A note on her front door. God knew how many of her neighbors saw it before she did. Her pride had yet to recover from that lethal blow.

"You okay?" Connell's concerned voice interrupted her musings, and she snapped back to reality with a jolt.

"I'm fine. Just wondering what lies ahead for us."

"I know what lies ahead."

"You do?"

"Yup, the replacement of those damned handcuffs, then a long bus ride followed by four weeks of sleeping on the ground, eating God knows what, and dancing at the end of some marionette strings for the entertainment of strangers cozied up on living room couches, all for the slim chance we'll win enough to get Majestic Health back in the black. Right?"

Sighing in defeat, she shrugged. "I guess so."

"Okay, then, let's go kick some Balinese jungle butt and win ourselves a million dollars!"

Chapter Seven

After a two-hour bumpy ride, the bus lurched to a stop at the side of a primitive road rutted with rocks and ditches.

"All right." Bart Meadows stood in the center aisle. "You will now be directed off the bus two-by-two. C'mon, people. Smile. You're supposed to be having fun."

"I'd like to tie him to an anthill, cover him with maple syrup, then tell him to smile 'cause he's supposed to be having fun," a gruff voice whispered behind Renata.

Holding back her laughter resulted in a loud snort, and she glanced at Connell. His tightened lips suggested he had the very same reaction.

"Everybody up!" Bart shouted, raising both hands palm up in the air. "Let's move out. From here, we walk. We're heading to a camp the production crew set up past the jungles in the north."

Keeping an eye on the purple mountains hovering in the distance, Renata and Connell stumbled through a wilderness far more dangerous in her mind than walking in Central Park at night. She clumsily trailed around moss-bearded trees and tripped over strangling vines. Together they scrambled over monstrous rocks glinting with bits of silver, and waded through narrow streams of rushing water.

At least the scenery forced Renata's mind off vivid daydreams about Connell. Pale lavender and gold-tipped white blossoms lying in the rich black earth, bordering the edges of streams, even growing out of tree branches, did more than catch her eye. They distracted from the artful grace with which Connell moved through the thick forest like a wild animal seeking prey.

Exotic and delicate orchids lent a bit of color and a touch of femininity to the rough jungle around them. Their fragrance filled the air, tickling her nose and swirling atop her tongue, helping her to forget her musings of the warm taste of his breath inside her mouth.

Her ears pricked at odd bird calls and the rustle of unknown creatures moving through thick underbrush. Snakes, rats, even the thought of giant spiders fueled her imagination. But the animals in this paradise hid from the human intruders, increasing Renata's innermost fears of Mother Nature at her creepiest.

Only heavy footfalls and boisterous conversations spoiled Bali's rugged, wild beauty. Rabid cameramen, nearly invisible in Kuta, hovered everywhere, lenses and blinding lights zooming in for close-ups like dive-bombing kamikazes.

After thirty stumble-bumble minutes of sloshing through streams, sinking into mud, and slapping away heavy wet leaves, Renata noticed the vines and stones of jungle life transform into atypical cables, wires and man-made machinery. Shiny silver trailers lay in a semicircle around a large open area, and beyond the trailers, a tranquil lagoon lent the site a Gilligan's Island aura. At last.

The Bonds of Matri-money campsite. She breathed a sigh of relief that they'd made it this far, but a queasiness remained deep in her belly.

Immediately upon reaching their destination, Bart Meadows announced the first challenge. "Each couple must pitch a tent for shelter. All tools required for the task are in the backpacks the men carry. You'll have thirty minutes. Those who do not have a suitable structure erected in that time will be disqualified and sent to Home Base at the Summerhouse Hotel." Holding a stopwatch in the air, he announced, "Ready? Set. Go."

Renata turned to Connell, nervousness blended with perspiration to drip down her back. "Do you know how to pitch a tent?"

"Simple enough. I was a Boy Scout for years. First, we have to look around a bit. We need to find the right location."

"How about over there?" She pointed to a nice, wide, flat piece of land beneath a low-hanging banyan tree. "Lots of shade and soft moss . . ."

"Nope. The ground is too flat."

"I thought we wanted flat ground." She tried to raise her hands to her hips, but the handcuff stopped her, and she settled for sarcasm to get her point across. "Or do you expect me to sleep on rocks for the next four weeks?"

"Forgive me, Princess. But ground that flat has been forced down from water. If it rains, we'll be lying in the middle of a huge puddle. We need a place with a small crown."

"Okay, sorry." Whipping her head from side to side, she scanned the area as if she knew what to look for, and then finally gave up. "Um, Connell? What's a crown?"

He shook his head and sighed. "You've never camped before, have you?"

"Up 'til now, my idea of roughing it has been staying at a three-star hotel instead of a four."

His eyes moved from her apologetic shrug to the canopy of trees above them. "Fabulous. Just follow my lead, okay?"

"You got it."

Within minutes, she regretted her acquiescence. He scanned the area like a dog sniffing out a convict, dragging her through two streams, over a hill and back before he found what he claimed was the perfect spot.

The tents provided by the television crew were standard camping issue, military green canvas attached to the ground with long stakes. It should have been easy for a carpenter with Connell's golden reputation to erect a shelter in no time. After taking the stakes and a mallet out of his backpack, he pulled her down to her knees beside him and handed her an iron peg.

"Here."

She turned it over, looking at it from several different angles before asking, "What am I supposed to do with this?"

With his free hand, he poked a hole in the soft ground. "Place the pointy end here and hold it tight. I'll do the rest."

"Don't talk to me like I'm an idiot, okay?"

"Sorry." His tone sounded remorseful, but the bemused grin he flashed said otherwise.

Biting her tongue, she stuck the pointy end of the stake into the hole and held it steady. Connell, with the mallet in his right hand as high as he could reach while on his knees, swung downward. Right smack dab on his left thumb.

"Dammit!"

"That's what you get for acting so smug," she told him, stifling a giggle.

"It isn't funny, Renata. Look at this." The nail hung from the side of his finger and bright red blood seeped through an open wound. Instantly, her nursing instincts took over.

"Take a break, Daniel Boone." She plopped the stake on the ground. "We've gotta get that fixed right away."

"I want to get the tent up first, Florence Nightingale," he retorted. "If you don't mind. It's just a small cut, for God's sake. It looks worse than it is."

"Well, I do mind. And I'm not holding a single tent stake or doing anything else to help until you let me treat that thumb. In this part of the world you run the risk of infection, gangrene, or God knows what else if you're not careful. How good a carpenter will you be with less than ten fingers?"

"Fine. Do that voodoo you do so well, but hurry up. I don't want to lose the first challenge and wind up back at Home Base."

Cupping her free hand to her mouth, she called, "I need the first-aid kit over here!"

With a rustle of leaves, a skinny, dark-haired production assistant came bounding through the thick foliage carrying a little white case with a red cross emblazoned on its side. "Here you go."

Renata took the case, her eyes never leaving Connell's wound. "Thank you." She opened the latch and pulled out a bottle of hydrogen peroxide, several cotton balls, and an adhesive bandage.

On second glance, the injury didn't look as serious as she'd originally thought, but she'd never give him the satisfaction of admitting he was right. Instead she fussed as if it were life-threatening, taking care to only use a few drops of peroxide at a time and ignoring his hiss of breath as the liquid bubbled around the open cut. After blowing a bit of air through pursed lips, she dabbed the area with the cotton until the bleeding stopped, then placed the bandage around the injured digit. When she finished, she held it up, grinning with pride at her magnificent demonstration of the healing arts. "There."

"Done?" He held the thumb in front of his face, pushing his lips into a full pout and knitting his eyebrows to form a childish expression. "No kiss to make it all better?"

"No," she said, yanking them to their feet and signaling the production assistant to remove the kit. "We have a tent to put up."

"You think you can help now?"

"I'm going to have to." She lifted her handcuffed wrist in the air, his naturally following suit. "Like it or not, you're stuck with me for the next month."

Connell picked up the mallet again, his cheeks heating. He liked being "stuck with" her. He liked it too much. He'd slammed his thumb because he'd been too distracted by her nearness, the smell of her, the sound of her voice, the thought that she stood no more than six inches from him and would probably remain there for the next thirty days.

Renata set the stake back in the ground as he raised the mallet above his shoulders.

"You ready?" he asked.

When he received her nod, he brought it down directly on the head of the stake. Sheer luck this time. Regardless of how hard he tried, his eyes strayed over her perfection, as if committing her to memory. Before lifting the mallet again, he took a moment to wipe the sweat from his brow with his bare arm. How could he ever hope to survive the next four weeks handcuffed to her?

Good God, this coming month would kill him. Why couldn't he be drawn to a woman who was drawn to him? Why did he always desire the ones who desired someone else? Was he one of those commitment-phobic men he saw decimated on women's magazine covers at the corner newsstand? No, that couldn't be it. He'd wanted to marry Annie; she hadn't wanted to marry him. But then again, maybe he chose Annie because, deep inside, he *knew* she wouldn't go through with the wedding.

Oh, he could blame Duncan publicly for stealing her, but the truth of the matter was he suspected she only wanted to marry him for the sake of being married. She was always more interested in the details of the wedding than in the details of the marriage. In retrospect, it was probably better he discovered her misgivings before they said "I do."

As for Renata, well, she was an incredible woman. A bit testy at times, but what good was rice without jambalaya? A little spice was sadly lacking in his life. Until now.

"Did someone over here call for the first-aid kit?"

With mallet in midair, Connell looked up from the stake straight into the concerned faces of Gilly and Clarice.

"Is everything okay with you guys?" Clarice asked.

Before he could stammer out a reply, Gilly answered his wife's question. "No, Clarice, everything's not okay. Can't you see they don't have their tent up yet? Let's go grab the other corner and help them out. You gotta get your tent up in the next ten minutes or you're on your way back to Home Base. Now, Connell, you and Renata finish pounding that stake into the ground, and Clarice and I will start on the opposite corner."

Serious now, Renata skooched closer to Connell and settled her right knee against his thigh. Sparks of electricity flickered in his veins, like a lightbulb sputtering just before going out.

One thing was for damn sure—he'd never survive to see one dime of the million-dollar prize . . .

Chapter Eight

The production staff escorted four couples to the bus after they failed the first challenge. Thanks to the assistance of their newfound teammates, Renata and Connell remained. Once the disappointed group left the campsite, the remaining thirty-two contestants divided into four teams with four couples each. The MacAllister and Tompkins duos joined a couple from Philadelphia, Roger and Trish Gardner; and a couple from San Diego, Bruce and Jennifer Bennett.

"You'll now need a name for your team," Bart instructed. "Something simple yet clever, preferably with a breed of animal prominently noted in it."

"Why not the Stupid Asses?" Roger mumbled. "I have a feeling we're going to regret going along with this brainless stunt before long."

"How about the Bali Llamas?" Connell suggested.

A murmur of appreciation broke out among the couples. "I like it," Gilly announced. "All those in favor, say 'aye.'"

"Aye!" reverberated through the group.

"Good, that's settled," Gilly said with a nod. "Hey, Bart, we've decided on the Bali Llamas."

"Yes, quite good," Bart replied. "Anyone else?"

"The Birds of Paradise," another woman shouted.

"The River Rats," a portly man to Renata's right offered.

"And we'll be the Diamond Rattlesnakes," a giggly voice called out. "Since we're all newlyweds. Get it? Diamonds?"

As if the sledgehammer she'd used hadn't already pounded the joke into the ground, the owner of the voice waved her hand in the air to show off the gigantic rock on her finger. Two carats at least, Renata thought as she stared agog. How could anyone wear something so vulgar? Especially here, living in the wilderness for a month? She should have left that headlight in the hotel safe in Kuta.

"Wonderful!" Bart enthused. Clearly, the man didn't get this job due to his intelligence. "Your next challenge is finding food for dinner. You'll have a daily allotment of rice, but that won't go far alone. Therefore, you must learn to spear fish in the lagoon at the edge of the campsite. The coral reefs are filled with small gold-speckled fish called sand gobies, a Balinese favorite. They're quite delicious when cooked . . ."

"I've heard of gobies," Bruce said in a low tone to the other Llamas. "We'll wrap them in banana leaves and cook them over a campfire. They'll be delicious."

"Bruce is the head chef in a four-star restaurant in La Jolla," Jennifer boasted. "If he says the meal will be delicious, you can believe him."

"But before you can cook them," Bart said, "you must figure out how to make a campfire with the accoutrements inside your backpacks. You have a knife, some string, and lip balm. Believe it or not, everything else you need to build a decent fire lies somewhere in your surroundings."

"Oh, great," Renata muttered. "Why don't we just give up now before we humiliate ourselves?"

Connell chastised her with a quick "Sssshhh!"

"If your team has the wherewithal to start a fire with these barest of necessities," Bart continued, "we'll reward you with five points and a supply of waterproof matches to use for the remainder of your stay. If you cannot start the fire without modern conveniences to assist you, you will lose five points. But you may still obtain the waterproof matches."

"How?" a man on the Birds of Paradise team asked.

Bart smiled, flashing those sickeningly pearly whites. "We'll simply ask that one couple from your team be sent back to Home Base in exchange for the matches. However, being one couple short might leave your team at a distinct disadvantage for future challenges. Therefore, it behooves you to succeed with nothing but your skills and common sense. I wish you all the best of luck."

After flashing a thumbs-up sign, he turned and headed for a shiny recreational vehicle set a short ways back at the edge of the clearing. Air-conditioning whirred noisily, and thick electric cables snaked around the ground near the trailer. The roof held a satellite dish and several radio antennae.

Nice digs, Renata thought. *Looks like the survival guru doesn't go without his twentieth-century luxuries, regardless of what the contestants are forced to endure. I'll bet good ol' Bart has a nice soft bed and a nice soft girl to go along with all his other creature comforts in that thing.*

"What are we going to do?" Clarice wailed, rummaging through Gilly's backpack with her free hand. "Does anyone know how to build a fire without matches or flint? These bags don't contain either."

"I do," Connell volunteered.

He does?! While Renata stared at him as if he'd suddenly grown two heads, Bruce stepped into the center of the circle of couples with Jennifer right beside him.

"Then it's settled. Jennifer and I will spear the gobies," Bruce announced. "Roger and Trish, you gather a whole lot of banana leaves, the bigger the better. And some of the fruits for dessert. Renata and Connell will collect the wood and prepare a fire. You sure you can handle it, MacAllister?"

Renata would have loved to see Connell "handle" the Californian with a two-by-four. To her disappointment, he only nodded. "Sure. No sweat."

"Excellent," Bruce exclaimed, his eyes swinging from Connell to her. "Because if you two don't get a fire started, we're sending you to Home Base in exchange for the matches."

She took a step forward. "I don't think—"

One quick yank on the handcuffs pulled her back to stand beside Connell. His brows knitted in that familiar "Don't say another word" glare, and she sent a stare right back at him.

Mental note: Once we're alone, we're going to have a little discussion about you treating me like a dog on a leash.

"Fair enough," she heard Connell tell Bruce.

She simmered, but kept her lips sealed tighter than a clam's.

"After you've got a fire going, Clarice and Gilly will cook the rice to go with the fish. Is everyone in agreement?"

Who did this four-star chef think he was? He'd taken the leadership position as if handed an order for an entree in his restaurant. And Renata didn't remember a waiter taking her preferences, much less seeing a menu. But if she did order something, she'd want it turned slowly on a spit . . .

Connell must have sensed the resentment brewing like hot coffee in her veins, because his voice advised in a low murmur, "Nope, he's not worth a million dollars either."

"Are you sure?" she asked. "It'd really make me feel good to put three years of kickboxing to use on his ribcage."

"Three years, eh?" Connell sounded impressed. "Much as I'd like to see that, I think we should hold on to our dignity for as long as possible. You ready?"

"Do I have a choice? I guess I should be grateful. After all, why prolong our agony, right? The sooner we fail, the sooner this farce will be over."

"What was that?" He leaned closer to hear her grumbles, and she instinctively took a step back, only to have the link of chain at her wrist bring her up short.

"Nothing."

"We can quit right now if you want." Connell's simple offer renewed some semblance of reality to her brain, and her mind chastised her in blistering tones.

Don't give up yet. You can't afford to surrender so easily. Remember why you're doing this. Remember the hospital stay so long ago. Remember how many people helped you, and your promise to repay that generosity. Remember Nana and what you owe her. You'll never accomplish anything without winning the money from this inane show. And you'll never win the money if you don't cooperate.

"Come on," she finally said, more to urge herself into moving forward than for Connell. "Let's gather firewood."

They headed away from the clearing and deeper into the forest, stepping over twisting vines and unearthed roots. Although the tall canopy of trees provided some shade from the powerful sun, the humidity overwhelmed her. Sweat trickled from her underarms down along to her wrists then pooled into her palms. Every inch of her skin itched with clammy dampness. She'd kill for a shower with a bar of rich, lathering deodorant soap.

"You realize, of course, we're going to have a tough time finding viable firewood here," Connell's voice intruded into her shower daydream. "It's pretty damp."

"Well, hey, thanks for speaking up about that when the Tyrant of Tiramisu ordered us to the task," she snapped. "Now if we don't succeed, we'll get booted to Home Base. On our first day, no less."

"Relax. Take it easy, Renata. I can do this. Trust me."

"I don't want to trust you. I don't want to trust anyone." She raked her free hand through her filthy hair in exasperation. Even thoughts of Nana couldn't calm the frustrations bubbling in the pit of her stomach. Put her faith in another man? Only an insane woman would consider such an idea. Hadn't Steve's departure taught her a valuable lesson regarding trust?

Plunge ahead, Renata. Don't give up.

"What is wrong with you?"

How could she possibly make him understand? She shook her head and sighed, releasing all her bad humors in one blast of air. "I don't know. The heat, I guess. I'm just not sure I'm cut out for all this pressure."

"Sure you are." He clasped their cuffed hands together to give her a reassuring squeeze. "You're a New Yorker, an ER nurse, and if that isn't enough stress, you're trying to get a charitable organization off the ground single-handedly. This place is a carriage ride through Central Park for someone with your drive and determination."

"No, it isn't." She kicked an errant rock in the moist,

black earth. It skittered across the ground for about two feet then plunked itself down in a soft depression, refusing to go any farther. Oh, to be a rock in this jungle and not go any farther than she wished. She already had her own depression, so that much was covered.

"C'mon, Renata. You're tougher than you think."

"I'm city girl tough. I do stuff like the hundred-yard dash across Fifth Avenue on the day after Thanksgiving. Or squeezing into a crowded subway car at rush hour. I can't handle this 'roughing it in the wilderness.' And then I complicate things by dragging you into my mess."

"You didn't drag me anywhere."

"I'm the biggest idiot on two continents. Don't ask me what I expected to happen when we got here. I don't know. I didn't expect handcuffs though. Bad enough I tied you to me in marriage. Now we're physically restrained. For a whole month." Her voice sank with her spirits. "You must hate me."

"I don't hate you."

"You should. I've been a witch since we got married."

"I hardly noticed." Was he kidding? She cocked an eyebrow at him. "Okay, I noticed a little. You wanna tell me why you've been a witch?"

"No." She looked at her feet, at the conifers and rope vines that covered the ground.

"Well, since you know you've acted like one, I can only assume it was deliberate on your part. For now, I'll let it go. But you know what? The way I see it, your attitude changes nothing. Either way, we're stuck together in this predicament. So let's make the most of it. Something tells me the challenges are going to get worse before they get better. And since we don't have love to keep us going, we have to rely on what we do have—a sense of humor. You think you can remember that?"

Without knowing why, she dropped her head to Connell's shoulder, almost as if she hoped to transfer her troubles to him, knowing he could bear them so much more easily. "I'll try."

"Good." He shrugged, bringing her head upright again. "But for now, keep your eyes up looking for firewood."

"Up? Don't you mean down?"

"No, I mean up. Anything on the ground is too wet to burn so we have to find dead wood still clinging to the trees."

"Dead wood, huh?" she replied thoughtfully. "Where's Steve when you need him?"

His laughter sent a flock of birds scattering into the highest tree branches with raucous screeches of indignation. "Atta girl! Come on, let's go kick some Balinese jungle butt and win ourselves a million dollars!"

If she'd known how tough their job would prove, she'd have put up more of a fuss at the outset. Finding dry wood in a tropical forest took sharp eyes and oodles of patience. By the time they returned to the campsite, perspiration soaked her from head to toe. The last thing she wanted now was to stand over an open fire. More than anything in the world, she craved a cleansing shower, her couch in her apartment in Queens, and a dish of soft vanilla ice cream.

But they had to build a fire. Without matches. No easy task for someone accustomed to flicking a switch for anything she needed. How did she get wrangled into this? And how could she wrangle out? With no other alternative, she simply followed Connell's lead, a practice quickly becoming habit for her, she thought with a little unease. But she pushed that uncomfortable idea far into the recesses of her mind then dropped it on the ground with her bundle of wood.

When he sank to his knees, she had no choice but to kneel beside him on the ground. Curiosity flared when he placed the assortment of odds and ends they'd gathered in a small pile around them. A bunch of twigs of various sizes, a tube of lip balm, a seashell, some twine, bits of feathers and fuzzies. For the life of her, she couldn't imagine how any of this junk would create so much as a spark, much less a fire large enough to cook fish to feed eight hungry people.

"Hand me that curved stick we picked up," he directed.

She held up a two-foot-long branch curved into a slight C. "This one?"

"That's it."

He took the bough from her, then reached behind his back for a length of string and tied it on each end of the branch, creating what looked like a bow for arrows.

"What are we going to do? Play Cowboys and Indians?"

"Just watch. You might learn something." He knelt on a flat piece of wood as he picked up a pointed stick, looping the string from the makeshift bow around it. "Take that lip balm they gave us and dab a little bit on the end of that seashell."

"Like this?" She squeezed a gob on the tip of the shell and smeared it around the edge with a finger.

"Yup. Now give them both to me."

She handed him the articles and sat back on her haunches to watch. First, he placed the gathered items atop the stick, which he set on the plank of wood. Then he drew the bowstring back and forth across the pile, sawing both their wrists in unison. He sawed faster and faster until sweat dripped down his face and onto the wood beneath him in coin-sized droplets. Her arm muscles soon ached with his efforts, and just as she was about to complain, something caught her eye. "Oh my God, I see smoke!"

"Didn't think your husband was so capable, did you?" He shifted his knee off the wood and placed a small bundle of dried bits of bark and animal fuzz in its place. Within minutes, the bundle sparked, then caught fire.

"You did it," she exclaimed. "I can't believe it."

He shrugged. "Of course. You shouldn't have doubted me. We Scots are pretty hardheaded. Once we set our minds on something, we don't let go too easily."

He gestured for her to stand, his eyes watching as the tiny bud of fire bloomed into a flower of flames. He then tossed a piece of kindling onto the small blaze, then another. The flames spat a few crackles of light and ignited into a full-blown blaze. "Okay, Gilly," he called. "You and Clarice can get started on the rice now."

The other couple approached holding a black iron pot and a small canvas bag.

"I'll be damned," Gilly exclaimed as he stared at the burgeoning fire with wide-eyed appreciation. "I think Clarice and I are awfully lucky to be on your team, Connell boy. You're a good man to have around."

A whisper of discomfort rustled from Renata's shoulders to her wrist. She was beginning to share that very same opinion about her husband. And she didn't like it one bit.

Chapter Nine

Two teams didn't produce the required fire and sacrificed a couple for the benefit of matches. But since the Bali Llamas did not share that misfortune, they turned their attention to other dilemmas. Eating together proved a real challenge. With Renata's right hand cuffed to him, Connell had no choice but to completely relax his left, allowing her to use their joined wrists to her own advantage. If he didn't watch her carefully, his fingertips would slap her in the chin whenever she opened her mouth to slide the fork in. After the third time, she punched him in the shoulder, just as he shoved a forkful of rice into his mouth. The tines scraped against the roof of his mouth, and the rice dribbled to the ground.

"I get the idea," he told her, regret at the untasted rice clouding his voice.

"Thank you."

After that reminder, he made a deliberate effort to avoid losing any more of his meager rations. Bruce hadn't lied about the flavor of the gobies, made subtle and slightly sweet thanks to the banana leaves. With their flaky consistency, he could easily imagine such an entrée on the menu in some of the finest restaurants in Manhattan.

After dinner, the eight people sat around the roaring fire, leaning against their mates and relaxing their half-filled bellies. As night darkened, the forest lay still and hushed until Clarice opened a conversation. "How'd you all meet?"

Clarice's big eyes bored into Connell over the flickering flames. He thought he might pass the buck to someone else, but a bright beam of light in the distance caught his attention. One of the multitudes of cameramen hid beneath a banyan tree, filming their discussion for posterity.

"I own a contracting business in New York," he began. "About three years ago, a beautiful woman with a heart of gold approached me with a business idea she wanted to get off the ground."

"Don't tell me," Clarice giggled, holding up a hand to interrupt. "The woman was Renata."

"The one and only. Renata works in an emergency room in New York City and sees a fair share of patients who, despite all the advances in medicine and technology, will never live independent lives again. She wanted a partner with building experience who'd be willing to help these patients make their homes handicap accessible at little or no cost for financially strapped families."

"And you took on the task?" Clarice asked.

He nodded. "I couldn't turn her down if I wanted to. She came traipsing into my office, looking like some adult version of Little Red Riding Hood in this drop-dead sexy outfit."

"Oh, yeah?" Roger's interest showed as he leaned forward, a wolfish smile on his angular face. "What kind of sexy outfit?"

Trish placed a hand on her husband's shoulder and

pulled him back to a normal sitting position. "Knock it off, Rog," she chastised in a whisper loud enough for everyone to hear.

"Well, I still wanna know," Gilly admitted, waggling his brows in Renata's direction. "What was she wearing?"

"A red and white striped button-down shirt, jeans and high-heeled red leather boots," Connell replied. "Around her neck, she had a heart-shaped ruby on a gold chain."

"It was a garnet," Renata corrected.

Connell shrugged. "Whatever. Anyway, Renata was the ultimate 'Lady in Red.' From her jewelry to her shoes, everything she wore was red. I remember thinking, if she stepped out on a highway, she'd stop traffic."

"That reminds me of what Jennifer wore when I first met her," Bruce interrupted. "She was the restaurant critic for a local newspaper . . ."

Renata sat cross-legged on the mossy ground, her eyes staring over the dancing red-orange flames as she pretended to listen to the other couples sharing their "how we met" stories. In reality, her mind traveled thousands of miles away from the here and now, to the day she first met Connell.

How could he remember the outfit she wore? She barely remembered it herself until he described it. What kind of man noticed such a mundane thing? If Steve had told the tale, she'd chalk it up to the fact that he still cared about her during those days. But Connell barely gave her a second glance that afternoon and never looked twice at her since. At least, that's what she'd always believed.

If he could recall the simple shirt and jeans she wore the day they first met, perhaps he wasn't as disinterested as he'd always pretended. Of course, she couldn't remember what he'd worn. Although to be honest, his work wardrobe never changed. If forced to do so, she could probably come up with a reasonable guess regarding his attire.

"Renata?" Clarice's voice cut through her thoughts like a meat cleaver through gelatin. "You're awful quiet. Tell us when you first knew you were in love with Connell."

The other ladies agreed, clapping their hands in rapid succession. "Ooh, yeah, Renata, tell us."

Her mouth dried up faster than a water droplet in the microwave as her mind started doing stunning imitations of Ralph Kramden's famous hesitation phrase, *Hemmeda, hemmeda, hemmeda.*

"W-when I fell in love with him?"

The women nodded, wide-eyed and eager to hear a romantic tale of a tender moment or a sentimental song or angels singing in the heavens as lightning bolts danced around them.

"Yeah. C'mon honey," Connell leaned close to place his head on her shoulder. "You can tell them. It's okay."

If she could shoot shards of glass out her eye sockets, Connell would be lying in the dirt, bleeding from a thousand tiny wounds.

"It was our first date. He looked so handsome in his very best suit, an Armani no less. No one had ever gone to so much fuss for me before. And when the date was over, he didn't want me to leave. He kept asking me to stay with him. But when I told him I had to go to work, he insisted he should accompany me. He didn't want to leave me alone. As if, even then, he knew we belonged together. That's when I knew Connell was special."

As the ladies released a collective sigh of "Ah . . ." she bent to place a chaste kiss against Connell's forehead. "Isn't that right, sweetie?"

"Smooth, Renata," he murmured in her ear. "Very smooth."

"Talk about smooth," she whispered with a lighthearted air she prayed hid the nervous fluttering in her belly. "You started it with that vivid description of my outfit the day you met me. Now *that* was a smooth lie."

"That wasn't a lie, per se. I don't recall when exactly you wore that getup, but I never forgot it. You looked like walking dynamite. I half-expected to see the words 'Danger—Explosives' plastered across your backside when you walked away."

She snorted back her giggles and received a strange look from Clarice. "Sorry," she mumbled. "Private joke."

When she looked at Connell, the expression in his eyes reflected pure relaxation. No worry lines, no tight lips, absolutely no hint of concern he might have let his true feelings about her show.

The idea whittling away at her brain bordered on lunacy. He couldn't be in love with her. It was too impossible to consider seriously. So why did she wish it was true?

Chapter Ten

No matter how hard she tried, Renata couldn't get comfortable in jungle surroundings. City noises: screeching car alarms, the loud arguments of the couple in the apartment next door, emergency sirens wailing through the streets, the distant bong of church bells, all routinely provided a soothing lullaby to help her fall asleep. Here in this tropical solitude, every flutter of leaves pricked her ears. Her active imagination pictured a wide assortment of hungry animals lying in wait outside her tent, licking their chops in anticipation of the tasty feast she'd furnish if she were foolish enough to step one small foot from safety.

God, how she missed New York and her overpriced two-room apartment with all its petty annoyances. She missed the continuous drip of the leaky faucet the super kept promising to fix, but never got around to. She missed the high-pitched whiz of planes from La Guardia and Kennedy flying overhead, rattling her windows and shaking the walls around her. Come to think of it, she missed having walls around her. She missed her soft mattress with its natural sway in the middle from excessive usage and the familiar yellowish scent of old age. Beneath her now, the ground was rock-hard, and a sharp stone dug into her right shoulder with piercing accuracy. Worse, the moldy smell of aging moss cloaked her nostrils, and she feared she'd never get the musty odor out of her hair.

She missed her noisy air-conditioner with its locomotive-like motor sputtering as it labored to cool her room at night. Here, humidity seeped into her pores, making her skin clammy from the top of her scalp to the bottoms of her ankles.

Add to her other concerns the fact that she lay on her back in a sack chained to a total stranger. The confines of the sleeping bag kept them wedged together so tightly, a toothpick couldn't fit between them. Okay, Connell wasn't a *total* stranger, but she knew very little about him. She could almost hear Nana's creaky voice telling her their positions represented an omen.

You see, innamorata? There is no longer a physical gap between you and your husband. Now, perhaps you should try to close the emotional one. After all, you are married. Even if it is a temporary union . . .

Renata's conscience took over the conversation from there. Connell seemed fairly open to developing a rapport. This tent gave them their only privacy to discuss anything personal. And she had to admit, she'd behaved badly for the last week. She'd give anything to turn back time and start again. But, maybe that wasn't really necessary. He'd already said he'd let her attitude slide. He'd obviously made his peace with her. Now she had to make her peace with him.

"Um, Connell?" She rose onto her left elbow, her right arm buried beneath his left in the confines encasing them both.

In the darkness she heard his shorts rustle against the nylon lining, suggesting he'd turned toward the sound of her voice. "Yeah?"

"Could we talk for a little while?"

Even in her own ears, she sounded like a child waking her parents after a nightmare. *How embarrassing! He probably thinks I'm afraid of the dark. Or the boogeyman.*

"What do you want to talk about?"

Shyness stole her reasoning, leaving her mind scrambling for something logical in a whirling dervish of nonsense. "I-I don't know. Anything."

"Just need to hear the golden strains of my voice, eh?" His deep chuckle filled the tent as he struggled to sit up. "I have a nephew like that. Three years old and he refuses to go to sleep 'til he hears the theme from *South Park*. His parents had to record it so they can play it before nine thirty every night."

She grasped for the topic thrown to her as if it were a life preserver. "You have a nephew?"

"Yup. My brother Duncan's boy."

"I don't know anything about you," she whispered, not daring to look in his direction as she spoke. "Except that I sandbagged you into marrying me just to get here."

"No one sandbags me into anything. What do you want to know about me?"

"Well, for starters, you have a brother?"

"I have two brothers and two sisters," he replied. "In order of oldest to youngest we are Connell, Duncan, Paisley, Stratton and Davina MacAllister."

"Paisley and Davina? Your poor sisters."

"Actually, Paisley is my youngest brother."

"You're joking!"

"Of course I'm joking. Paisley is my little sister."

"Are you close to all your siblings?"

"Usually."

In an instant, the smooth tone hardened to steel, and the silence following his terse reply roared through her ears like a typhoon. Odd how in the dark her other senses became more alert, more conscious of the nuances in his ever-changing moods. Not that the shift compared to a nuance. This was a physical change, impossible for the most insensitive clod to miss. "Tell me about your nephew."

Again, the change was instantaneous. And nerve-wracking. She could actually hear his indulgent smile as the mellow tone returned, and the air around them lightened from oppressive to breathable. "His name is Kiernan. Kiernan Aramis MacAllister. He turned three in April."

"What-an What-amis?"

He chuckled. "I know; it's a ridiculous name. But you have to understand. My parents are very proud of their Scots heritage. It's sort of a tradition to give ancestral names to the kids in the MacAllister family. Mom and Dad expect each of us to carry it on with our own children. My sister-in-law was willing to keep the peace, but she wanted something of herself in Kiernan. That meant Aramis."

"I'm confused. Why would Aramis represent her? Isn't that a cologne?"

"Originally, Aramis was one of the Three Musketeers. Annie always had a thing for old black-and-white movies. She'd rent 'em by the dozens. Her favorites were the swashbucklers. *Captain Blood, The Adventures of Robin Hood, The Mark of Zorro, The Three Musketeers.* One night, we had a Douglas Fairbanks and Errol Flynn marathon. We stayed up all night watching—"

We. Alarm bells rang feverishly inside her head at the

laissez-faire way he said that simple pronoun. As if it shouldn't mean anything, but strangely, she knew it did. "We" spoke volumes to her. And she didn't like the connotations it brought to mind.

"You said, '*We* had a marathon.' Do you mean, you, Duncan, and Annie? Or just you and Annie?"

"What difference does it make?"

Bingo! Pay dirt. "You tell me."

"What does *that* mean?"

"What's with you and Annie?"

"Nothing. Let it go, Renata."

A long time ago, someone she knew had described an overly tense moment as an elephant in the room that no one dared mention or address. But this wasn't just an elephant inside their tent; this was a brontosaurus. And its name was Annie.

"Forget it," she said, her courage fading in the face of the imagined dinosaur settling its staggering weight on her chest. "Forget I mentioned anything."

"Gladly." She felt a tug on her wrist then heard a crisp rustle suggesting he'd slid into the sleeping bag and turned his face away from her.

Silence permeated the tent again, leaving her to wonder what she'd learned in their brief conversation. Not much. And yet, more than she would have liked. With a shake of her head, she scooted back down into a reclining position, staring at the shadowed points of the tent above her.

So Connell had the hots for his sister-in-law. Did his brother know? Was that the reason for the obvious tension between the siblings? Poor Duncan! She didn't even know the guy and she felt sorry for him. How did he stand the fact that competition for his wife's affection came from his own brother?

Must be some stiff competition. After all, Connell was

gorgeous. He had a great sense of humor and a smile that made her weak in the knees. What woman in her right mind would choose someone else over him?

Or was Connell the runt of the MacAllister litter? The ugly duckling? Impossible. The man was close to perfect. If Duncan were a better man in the slightest, she'd have seen his face gracing the cover of a thousand magazines as Bachelor of the Month. And good ol' Annie wouldn't have lassoed him without a fight from the throngs of single gals in the New York metropolitan area.

So what would make Annie choose Duncan over Connell? Because as sure as she knew her name, Renata Jacqueline Moon MacAllister knew Connell's familial animosity came from the fact he'd lost Annie to his brother.

"Renata?" Connell's subdued voice broke into her thoughts. "I'm sorry. I overreacted and I'm sorry."

A gorgeous man who was big enough to apologize? Boy, if she ever met this Annie, she'd slap her upside the head for throwing away the treasure she'd been offered. What an idiot!

"Forget it, Connell," she murmured, moving closer to him. "Go to sleep."

He rolled onto his side facing her. Soft, warm breath fell upon her nose and cheeks in even intervals. His light puffs of air skittered across her neck and down her spine in ripples, like throwing a rock across the surface of a still pond. Pangs of guilt clawed upward from her belly to meet the wavelets, leaving her torn between wanting to fall asleep as quickly as possible and wanting to talk to him all night. They'd only called a truce to their arguments earlier this morning. Why destroy that precarious peace with a misunderstanding about a woman thousands of miles away from the here and now?

As if sharing her reluctance to end the night on a sour note, he broke the silence. "What about you?"

She shrugged. Then, realizing he couldn't see her, replied, "I'm not used to sleeping outdoors. But don't worry; I'll fall asleep eventually."

"No, I meant what about your family? How many brothers and sisters do you have?"

"None."

"I bet every kid with siblings has wished to be an only child at one time or another. Lucky you lived that dream for us."

"No, I didn't. Not really."

"Oh? What does that mean, not really?"

"Nothing. Let it go, Connell."

In a sneaky attempt to make her explain herself, he poked her between the ribs. "You are being foolish," he threatened in a mock German accent. "Ve have vays to make you talk."

She screeched her outrage, but soon melted into a fit of giggles as he prodded her waist and underarms with wiggling fingers. "Stop! Stop it!"

"Not until you tell me what you meant."

"Never," she managed through paroxysms of laughter.

He rose on an elbow to lean over her squirming body, and his flattened palm caressed her bare arm in long, slow movements. Currents of electricity crackled around them. The ripples she'd felt moments ago escalated to a fierce undertow, pulling her closer, closer . . .

The cursed handcuffs now became a benefit; she couldn't run away even if she wished. In slow motion, she raised her neck, and he seized the opportunity she gladly offered, clamping his lips over hers in a vice-like grip.

She'd never breathed until this moment. All her life she'd inhaled and exhaled without thinking. When his mouth clung to hers, she drew him into her lungs one molecule at a time. Inch by blissful inch, his kiss expanded her ribcage until her chest broadened like a balloon filling with helium, making her float.

"Rennie," he murmured. "God, I've waited so long to hold you this way."

Did he just say Annie?

He must have; he couldn't possibly have longed to hold her. He'd never desired her before this moment. At the humiliating thought that he'd called out another woman's name, the helium deflated. Reality returned with a headlong plunge from her precarious height to the ground below.

"Rennie?" His husky voice attempted to call her back into his embrace, but the passion had frozen in her veins.

"It was a mistake," she said in a tone more frigid than her blood. "Forget this ever happened."

"What if I don't want to forget?" His shadowy form sat up. "What's wrong?"

"Nothing's wrong. Go to sleep."

"Rennie, I—"

"Stop calling me that! My name is Renata, not Rennie."

"Whatever you say, *Renata.*" He inflected her name as if addressing her as "Your Majesty."

Her heart barely took notice of his sarcasm, too lost in its own misery to care about his.

He rolled over onto his side, pulling her arm with him, and muttered a terse, "Good night."

If only . . .

Chapter Eleven

The following morning, through eyes drier than the Sahara at noon, Renata faced a sea of smiles and sparkling eyes. The marital happiness displayed by the other couples only served to punctuate Renata's misery. She still wasn't one hundred percent certain which name Connell had said last night. Pride wanted to believe it was hers, but stubbornness told her it was Annie's.

Anyway, why should it matter? Aside from the natural discomfort such a situation brought, of course. She wasn't in love with Connell. So what did she care if he had a thing for his sister-in-law? She didn't own him. She didn't even want him.

To prove it, she focused her attention on Bart Meadows' emotive drone. "Today, we'll travel to the Gitgit waterfall near Singaraja. It's a popular tourist attraction, over forty meters high and quite lovely. It even has a pool at the bottom for swimming. Though I must warn you, legend says couples who swim there together are destined to separate."

A grumble went through the crowd of newlyweds who

wavered between the imagined heaven of cool water cleansing their overheated, dirty flesh versus the superstition rearing the specter of divorce among them.

"As you trek through the jungle to the waterfall, you ladies will balance this on your heads, just as the natives do with everything from food to furniture." He held a backpack wrapped in bungee cords high in the air for all to see. "At no time will you be allowed to touch the backpack with your hands, although your husband may. You may not speak to one another. It will be up to you to maintain communication simply by your knowledge of one another's movements and moods."

Oh, great. Connell and I have done such a fabulous job communicating with one another so far.

"If you make it to the waterfall without dropping your burden, your team will receive ten points." Bart's overinflected tone set Renata's frazzled nerves rolling to the edge of her spine like ducks in a shooting gallery. "But each time you drop the backpack, one point will be deducted from your team's total score. If your score should decrease to a negative number—that is, less than zero—" Renata rolled her eyes in exasperation at that tidbit of wisdom, "—your team will be disqualified from competition and sent to Home Base."

"You're so lucky you've got a flat head," Clarice said to her, poking her in the ribs. "You'll be able to balance okay."

Her teetering nerves took the downward plunge. Since when did she have a flat head? At the sound of a loud snort, she whirled to face Connell. His shoulders hunched up and down as he resisted the urge to laugh out loud. Her fingers curled into fists as she resisted the urge to punch him.

"Clarice, honey," Gilly interjected. "I don't think Renata liked hearing that."

"Oh, c'mon, Gilly. She knows what I mean. She's got a square-ish shaped face so the top of her head's flat. Especially now with her hair all matted down."

"Somehow I don't think you're making things any better," Connell said through snorts.

While the others swallowed insipid smiles, the urge to hit someone or something flared in Renata, and she dug her nails into her palms, leaving little crescent moons in their wake.

"Besides," Connell continued, his eyes staring at her with heated intensity, "I think she looks terrific."

The tropical heat must have affected him more seriously than anyone realized. Had he picked up some bizarre jungle fever that diminished his mental capacity?

Even without a mirror, she could predict what she looked like after two days without a shower and a night with no sleep: hair plastered to her head like a military helmet, rings as large as Saturn's framing her sunken bleary eyes, sweat beading on her forehead and the edges of her cheeks. Yup, she was a raving beauty, all right.

Before she could reach a hand to his forehead to check his temperature, a production assistant shoved one of the heavy backpacks at her. She would have stumbled if Connell hadn't grabbed her elbow to steady her. And that set her mind thinking.

Maybe they could communicate without words after all . . .

"Let's head out!" Bart announced with an upraised hand signaling a gesture more indicative of the leader of a cattle drive than a game show host.

Three hours later, plodding over concrete steps toward the Gitgit waterfall, Connell did his damnedest to keep his eyes on the backpack atop Renata's head. Unfortunately, the memory of last night's kiss refused to stay in the background.

She'd tasted sweet and piquant, like dark chocolate. He loved dark chocolate—the way it melted on his tongue, pooling in his throat until sheer pleasure flowed like a river inside his mouth. Oh, yeah. Renata was dark chocolate, all right. But, he'd moved too fast and scared her off.

Her breakup with Steve was too fresh. He needed to take his time and savor her the way she deserved to be savored. Let her see he wasn't some Neanderthal looking for any woman to satisfy a lustful impulse. The last thing she probably wanted right now was a man whose testosterone levels ran higher than his IQ.

She tripped over an upturned step then, pitching forward against him. The subtle contact sent a new jolt of liquid heat into his bloodstream. But he had the presence of mind to catch the backpack before it slid off her head and onto the ground.

He gave her what he hoped was an encouraging smile as he replaced the bundle atop her flat head. She frowned, and he fought the urge to laugh. Regardless of the expression of disapproval she wore, she couldn't intimidate him. Especially now when she appeared as dangerous as a stuffed animal.

Her soft brown eyes, though swollen and red-rimmed from lack of sleep, held the same innocence as Kiernan's Paddington Bear. Still, Paddington did have the advantage of being fairly clean. With her black hair hanging limply around sweat-stained cheeks, the top of her head flattened, just as Clarice had pointed out earlier. Maybe that was why she managed to keep the backpack in place while all the other contestants had dropped theirs at least once. Or maybe it was the way she walked. With head held high and shoulders thrown back, her stride exuded supple grace—a fashion model doing a turn on the catwalk.

Flat head or not, in his eyes, she looked more beautiful than some skeletal fashion model. Even the plainest woman might resemble a goddess with the right clothes, the perfect hairstyle, and a truckload of makeup. Renata's features didn't need such enhancements. She was perfect the way she was. Without any of the accoutrements a woman normally used to entice a man; no perfume, no high heels to make her legs look longer, no miracle underwear. Renata shone with more brilliance than a thousand suns. And God help him if he didn't want to bask in her radiance until he burned to ash.

Forcing his mind to concentrate on anything but Renata's alluring femininity, he listened to the rumbling water grow louder as they continued their trek. Due to the enforced silence between the couples, the cascade echoed like a roaring wind. Yet it never stirred the dracaena and philodendrons around them.

A rustle of leaves signaled the flight of beautiful white birds with lacy crests upon their heads and waves of electric blue across their eyes. They flew into open patches of azure sky, calling to one another as they soared. Their cries resounded through the forest like a rusty saw cutting through a thick plank of wood, and he winced at the series of dull groans followed by high-pitched squeals piercing his eardrums. God must have a weird sense of humor. Why else would He design a creature so beautiful, but give it a song more abrasive than the AFLAC duck with a headcold?

For that matter, why else would He force me into confinement with a woman I could really care about, if she didn't merely see me as a means to an end?

The humid, sticky air held a pungent smell difficult to

describe. Sweet mud—slightly spicy, slightly musky, slightly cinnamony all at the same time. He couldn't put his finger, or his nostrils, on the scent. Then they passed through the jungles and out into the open. Above them and on every side, deep green leaves tipped with blossoms of pink and yellow posed in the foreground. Up ahead, coffee trees and clove plants surrounded multi-tiered acres of rice paddies in definitive lines like a giant labyrinth. Coffee and cloves—that explained the exotic aroma filling the air.

A wizened farmer standing in the middle of a water-bogged rice field removed his wide-brimmed hat as they passed, waving it in greeting. Connell wondered what the old man must have thought about a conga-line of fourteen mute, handcuffed couples climbing their way to the waterfall. Whatever went through the stranger's mind, his smile remained broad and welcoming until they passed out of sight.

They plundered on, back into the thick of the jungle, and a rutted trail littered with uprooted vines and twisting branches replaced the concrete steps. Renata, walking in front of him, slowed her pace as she tried to keep the backpack steady on her head while her gaze skimmed the ground ahead for any possible dangers to maintaining her poise. Connell gave the inside of her palm a quick tickle with an index finger to remind her he was by her side, prepared to help in any way. She never made a motion to let him know she understood his silent message, but she did speed up again.

As they continued on, the rushing water's roar intensified in his ears, and a gentle mist descended on the broad green leaves, cooling his fevered flesh when it landed upon him. At last, they had arrived at the viewing point for the famous Gitgit waterfall.

But the proliferation of souvenir stalls and public toilets lining either side of the path diminished his first observation of the natural beauty itself. Shop owners and vendors descended upon the new crowd of tourists like a swarm of vultures, clamoring to sell their overpriced tchotchkes and doodads. For once, Connell appreciated the hovering production team. They batted the swarm away with upraised hands and terse head shakes.

When the sea of eager faces finally parted, a free-form cloud floated in the middle of the forest. It hovered just in his field of vision for a brief second and then slowly sank out of sight. And as the cloud descended the precipice of steep rocks, another emerged behind it, then another and another. The clouds weren't clouds at all. It was the waterfall, tumbling over the cliff in filigreed white shrouds to land in the broad blue-gray lagoon below.

Quick as a flash, Renata dropped the backpack on the ground with a thud. They'd passed their third challenge. Another step closer to the million dollar prize . . .

Reveling in their victory, they grinned with pride and displayed thumbs-up signs until the babble of the lagoon beckoned to Connell's tired sweaty body, coaxing him to swim. He took a step forward, entranced by the idea of soothing his burning skin in fresh icy water. Regardless of anyone else's feelings on the matter, he'd risk the anger of some local legend to find refreshment there.

Besides, he and Renata had a business arrangement, nothing more. Once this game show ended, they'd separate anyway. So what was the harm? A quick glance at the other couples told him where the harm lay. Every one of them stared at the lagoon as a starving man might look upon a crust of bread. Yet no matter how enticing, none moved closer to the edge. No one wanted to risk losing his or her mate for a few minutes' comfort.

The other contestants' circumstances contrasted so sharply with his and Renata's. These were people who'd vowed to love, honor, and cherish each other 'til death did them part. Yet while he and Renata had spoken the same vows, their reality was "'til a million dollars did them part." At this moment, he envied the couples who'd already returned to Home Base. With love on their side, they were far richer than he and Renata would ever be. He hoped they knew that.

"Never fear," Bart Meadows suddenly announced in a poor Robin Hood accent, "you'll all have the chance to swim without worrying about the Balinese legend. We'll temporarily separate you from your bonds. The ladies will swim first, followed soon after by the gentlemen. Your backpacks carry a change of clothing for afterward."

Sure enough, Mr. Lester appeared out of nowhere with his magic keys. He strode into the throng of couples and unlocked Connell's wrist from Renata's with a simple twist.

"We will continue to enforce the rules of silence," Bart reminded them. "Anyone who speaks will lose another point for their team."

The minute Mr. Lester released their hands, Renata walked to a bench beneath a nearby pavilion and removed her boots and socks. Barefoot, she dipped a toe into the water, and her breath escaped in a drawn-out hiss. The smile she wore as she waded into the pool jolted him like lightning.

Watching the ladies swim, Connell recalled an illustration of the Mermaid Lagoon in Kiernan's Peter Pan book. One mermaid in particular captured his attention. The mists surrounding the waterfall lent her a surreal beauty, like Aphrodite rising from the sea.

Now, more than ever, he'd need that icy cold swim. As soon as possible.

Chapter Twelve

That evening, after another dinner of gobies and rice, Clarice opened a new discussion for the couples. "What's your special song?" Her gaze settled on Connell and Renata first. Connell supposed she saw herself as the Bali Llamas' answer to Oprah Winfrey.

Renata had no reaction to the question. Her lids fought a losing battle to keep her eyes open. A stab of pity pierced his chest at the pathetic look on her face. Today's activities had taken their toll. She'd come in first in the challenge, but her restlessness last night combined with the exertion of the climb up to the waterfall today had sapped the last of her strength.

"Connell?" Clarice prompted.

"Um, sorry, Clarice, but Renata looks like her head's about to fall into the fire. I think we'll say good night for now."

"C'mon, chicken," Roger rejoined. "Or are you afraid you'll get it wrong?"

"Trust me, Roger. I wouldn't get it wrong. But if it satisfies your curiosity, our song is Etta James' 'At Last.'

Now if you'll excuse me, I'm going to take my wife to bed."

"Not a bad idea," Gilly purred, snaking an arm around Clarice's waist. "Something about being in the jungle brings out the animal in Clarice too."

"Gilly!" Clarice protested a little too hard.

Connell didn't stick around to see how their repartee turned out. Renata provided him with a more interesting dilemma. When he attempted to bring her to her feet, her body sagged against his chest as limp as old lettuce leaves. Her knees refused to lock into an upright position any more this evening. How could he get her to their tent without sacrificing her dignity and proving his Neanderthal tendencies by slinging her over his shoulder?

"I could take her feet if you want," Roger interjected.

Connell swallowed a grimace. God, the man was a total sleaze. "No, I'll take care of her, thanks."

"Poor thing's tuckered out, ain't she?" Clarice remarked.

Something in Clarice's voice awakened Renata. "I'm up," she protested weakly. "I'm okay."

"Quick," Roger exclaimed. "Renata, what's your wedding song?"

" 'At Last' by Etta James," she murmured.

If Connell had been a rooster, he would have crowed his delight. Instead, he threw a smug grin Roger's way and tossed Renata's arm over his shoulder. "Come on, sweetheart. Let's put you to bed."

He managed to drag her into their tent and set her atop the sleeping bag with only slight discomfort to his own wrist in its position bent halfway across his shoulder.

"How did you know that?" she mumbled.

"Know what?" he asked, unlacing her boots.

"My favorite song?"

"I thought you were sleeping."

"So did I. Until I heard Clarice pestering you. So how'd you know I love that song?"

"Beats me. You must have mentioned it."

She accepted the lie with no qualms, thank God. The truth would only upset her. Because the truth was he knew every one of her likes and dislikes. He knew she loved Etta James and the smell of the city after a rainstorm. She loved to cook, she had a great singing voice, and vanilla was her favorite scent. She enjoyed Broadway shows and Sunday's *New York Times* crossword puzzles. Her dislikes included espionage movies and gangsta rap. She found New Year's Eve depressing, but still loved to celebrate her birthday with childlike anticipation.

Over the last three years, Connell had catalogued every fact he could discern about her. In the beginning, he sought the flaw in her perfection—something that might leave a bad taste in his mouth. No such flaw existed. Soon, every mention of Steve's name hammered a nail into Connell's heart. There he stood in the center of some bizarre love triangle, secretly wanting her, and knowing she belonged to someone else.

"Connell?"

"Yeah?" His voice was unintentionally gruff.

"Do you really think we can pull this off?"

"Sure." He turned to look at her, but the darkness of the tent precluded seeing much of anything. "I thought you were tired. Go to sleep."

"I can't."

"You wanna talk some more? Why don't you tell me about your family tonight since we spoke about mine last night?"

"There isn't much to tell. It's just Nana and me."

"Nana the cat? That's it? No parents, no siblings, no one?"

"Just Nana and me," she repeated softly.

"Must be awfully lonely around the holidays."

"Especially Christmas."

"I bet."

He thought about Christmas with his own family. Since his parents sold their house and moved to Florida, Duncan and Annie hosted the celebration each year. All the traditions remained the same: smells of pine, mincemeat, and roast beef scenting the air, the music of Nat King Cole and Bing Crosby wafting in from the living room, an enormous tree glittering with lights and ornaments, colorful packages of every shape and size piled beneath. Mom and Dad flew up every year so the entire family celebrated together, filling the MacAllister house with laughter and love.

He never realized how fortunate he was until he compared his visions of the holiday to an imaginary picture of a quiet afternoon in Renata's apartment with nothing but a cat to keep her company. And maybe the old lady with her pet cockatiel stopping by long enough to tell stories of her torrid love affair with John F. Kennedy. No one to cook for, no one to buy presents for, no one to sing carols with. How painful for someone like Renata who loved those activities so much. Well, this year he'd remedy that.

According to his family's long-standing tradition, no one they knew ever spent the holiday alone. Those with nowhere else to go were always welcome at the MacAllister home. His mother said these special guests represented the spirits of deceased loved ones and should be greeted with warmth and affection. So when December 25 rolled around this year, he'd bring Renata with him.

He might have to drag her kicking and screaming, but no one should be alone on Christmas.

While his thoughts drifted, Renata finally dozed off.

Day Four began when a production assistant called from outside the tent flaps. "Mr. and Mrs. MacAllister? Are you awake?"

At the sound of a strange voice only a few feet away, Renata jerked upright, kicking at the sleeping bag restricting her legs. Her heel slammed against Connell's shin with enough power to leave a perfectly round bruise. "Ow! Dammit, Renata. When I asked to see your kickboxing skills, I didn't mean for you to use them on me. Wait a minute, and I'll get us out of this thing."

"I'm sorry," she snapped, yanking at the zipper. "It was a reflex. I'm not used to having strange men wake me."

"Neither am I," he retorted.

She stopped pulling at the zipper and stared at him, studying his face for any hint of a smile. Like giant scissors, his legs shot out to cover hers, pinning her in place.

"Hey!" she exclaimed. "What the—"

"Just hold still and let me get us out of this thing."

Renata bit her tongue to keep from telling him off. Who died and made him boss of this operation? Still, he *was* closer to the zipper than she was. So, okay, fine, she'd concede this time. "You've got thirty seconds, pal."

Connell struggled and pulled until, finally, the zipper released, and they managed to wriggle free to stand upright. Together, they hobbled over to the flap. Connell pushed it open with his free hand. "What is it?"

A young dark-haired assistant handed Renata two small pieces of yellow cloth. "You'll need these for this

morning's challenge, ma'am. You're to change your clothing, and be at the lagoon in fifteen minutes. Understand?"

"Yes, of course," she murmured.

With a nod, the assistant turned away from the tent.

"What is it?" Connell asked her.

She stared at the two scraps in her hand, then at the
retreating back of the assistant, then back at her hand
again. "I think it's a bikini. They want me to wear a bikini now?"

"It's for a million dollars," he reminded her quickly.

She shook her head in dismay. "Am I that transparent?"

"You are to me. But then again, I'd do anything short
of murder to see you in that getup. Something tells me
you're gonna look fantastic."

He gave her a wolfish smile, indicative of their team-
mate Roger's antics, and she laughed despite her discomfort. His attitude always lightened her mood when problems cropped up in this game. She wondered if he han-
dled concerns in the real world with the same aplomb and
skewed bit of humor he used here. His was a refreshing
change from her old worry wart behavior. But she refused
to pursue that avenue at the moment.

"So? You gonna put it on, or are we giving up already?"

She twirled a finger at him. "Turn around. Just because
you gained my quick cooperation in wearing this dental
floss doesn't mean you get a sneak preview."

"Hot dog! She's gonna put it on."

He clapped his hands as he spun around. The minute his
back faced her, she stripped off her shorts and panties. As
she knelt to pull them off her ankles, he instinctively followed her movements without turning around. She then slid
into the tiny string bikini bottoms and tugged them up,
Connell's movements mirroring her own.

She never feared he might peek at her while she was

vulnerable and exposed. He was too much of a gentleman for that, and she knew it. Strange how constant proximity had given them a newfound respect for each other. Thinking of how far they'd come in such a short time filled her with pride, and she smiled before turning her attention to the bikini top.

She managed to untie the halter, but tying the bra with only one hand proved too much for her to handle. "Um, Connell?"

"I know," he said, still facing the canvas walls around them. "You turn around, and I'll tie you up."

She giggled. "Sorry. It just sounds so ridiculous."

"Never mind," he growled. "Turn around."

She did so. When his hands grasped at the strings of the bra, she released her hold and lifted her hand to scoop her hair off her neck. The strings tightened around her nape first, then the middle of her back. His fingertips brushed against her flesh like feathers, light and ticklish, and she shuddered.

"Don't tell me you're cold."

"God, no! In this heat? Why on earth would you think that?"

His warm breath danced across her bare shoulder, converging with her own flush of embarrassment. Instant and overpowering fire flooded her from head to toe. The humid weather must have caused her reaction. If she stayed here a year, she'd never become accustomed to the tropical heat. It crushed her inch by inch, leaving her gasping for every breath she took.

"All done," he announced. "Are you okay? I thought I felt you shiver."

Dropping her hair down, she took a step away from him, as far as the handcuffs would allow. "Well, you didn't." She couldn't look at him when she told the lie.

She preferred to concentrate on the minimal material she wore. Who knew she'd miss the halter and short shorts she'd previously despised? Leave it to the executives of Maximus Productions to find a way to show even more skin on this damned show. A bikini, for God's sake. Could it get much worse?

For some odd reason an old song Grampa used to sing played inside her head. Something about a woman afraid to come out of the water in her "itsy bitsy, teeny weeny, yellow polka-dot bikini." As a child she'd found the song silly, but now she frowned as she realized the truth in the lyrics.

"You sure you're okay?" he persisted.

"We should get out to the lagoon. Who knows? They might dock us ten points if we're a minute late."

"Before we go, there's one thing I have to say."

"What?"

A grin encompassed his entire face. "I knew you'd look fantastic in that getup."

Chapter Thirteen

"Ready?"

At Renata's nod, Connell adjusted the snorkel in his mouth and ducked below the placid surface of the turquoise lagoon. Renata's legs kicked in knife-like precision right beside him.

Snorkeling for a key to a treasure chest. How ridiculous. Still, at least he got his first glimpse of Renata in a bikini. He supposed the producers insisted on the bathing suit to gain a bigger audience with the male demographic. He didn't have to be a Hollywood mogul to figure that much out. But if Renata's appearance affected millions of men watching this at home, how was he supposed to feel handcuffed to her side night and day?

Forcing his brain back to the problem at hand, he scanned the sugar-white sand floor of the lagoon, seeking a large brass key that hopefully fit the lock of a treasure chest on shore. Bart had explained that each couple must return with one of the keys anchored beneath the water. One unfortunate couple would not find a key; they would

111

return to Home Base. Only one key would open the treasure chest's lock. And the lucky couple who found *that* key would win an additional ten points for their team and immunity from banishment for the rest of the game. That was a prize well worth the effort, in his humble opinion. It guaranteed that, unless they did something stupid, they'd make it to the final round.

Through the diver's mask, he moved his gaze left to right and right to left as they swam in the marked area. But with all the other couples doing the same, they stirred up too much of the sand on the bottom, clouding the water and his vision. He yanked on Renata's wrist to signal they ascend again.

"It's no use," he said when they bobbed along the surface together. "There's too much activity to see anything."

"We don't have a choice. We need to find a key, or we'll screw the entire team, not to mention ourselves."

"I know, but I don't think we'll find it this way."

"Then what do you suggest?"

Odd. He didn't hear the sarcasm he'd come to expect from her. A choir of angels broke into hallelujah as the fact struck his subconscious. She probably wouldn't admit it yet, but she trusted him. And that was a tremendous step for her. The very idea made him buoyant. He thought he might walk on the water.

With a grin he couldn't hide if he'd tried, he asked, "Did you ever go clamming?"

"No."

"When we were kids, Dad used to take us out in the Great South Bay, and we'd dig for clams with our feet. It's fairly easy to do. We'd walk in very short steps, almost shuffling really, pushing our toes, then our heels into the sand until we felt something hard. Then we'd call to Dad and tell him where to look. You know, 'under my right big toe,' or, 'beneath my left heel.' He'd dive into the water to retrieve what we found. You and I could use the same method to find a key. The water's just about chin level here, certainly not too high for us to wade rather than snorkel. What do you think? Are you game?"

She shrugged. "Why not? Anything beats trying to find it from atop the surface. Let's do the Lost Key Shuffle."

He chuckled. There was that sense of humor popping up again. "Good one, Rennie." Oops. He forgot. He wasn't supposed to call her that. "I'm sorry. I know I shouldn't have, but it suits you. And it just slipped out—"

"It's okay," she assured him. "I don't mind if you use the name." Her eyes bored into his, trapping him as neatly as an insect in amber. "You can call me Rennie if you prefer. As a matter of fact, I kinda like the way you say the name."

"Why? How do I say it?"

"Like it means something special to you," she admitted, her voice a husky whisper. "Not just as a shortened version of my name, but as a . . ." She flicked the water with her fingertips, and droplets sparkled beneath the burning sunlight. ". . . I don't know. I'm stupid. Forget I mentioned anything."

"For the record, you don't sound stupid. I think I know what you mean."

"You do?"

"Mmm-hmm. But for now, it's time to get back to business. Thirteen keys sit somewhere beneath our feet, enough for every couple but one. Take off your flippers and we'll start the shuffle."

"Ready when you are." She held up the bright yellow fins.

"Good. Do what I do, and you'll be fine."

He took a few steps forward, scuffling his feet to catch

the first layer of sand and sift it with his toes. Renata followed suit. Occasionally, her toes brushed up against his foot, causing him to start suddenly.

"Sorry," she murmured when it happened for the third time in as many minutes. "I guess I'm not as experienced in this sort of thing as you."

"No sweat."

A few steps farther, something hard brushed against the ball of his foot. "Was that you again?"

She turned her gaze to him, hope glimmering in her eyes. "No. Do you think we found one?"

"Only one way to find out. Stay here. I'll be right back."

He left his fins to float along the surface, shoved the snorkel back into his mouth, slid the mask over his eyes, and plunged into the water. Using great care to keep from shifting the object from its hiding place, he crouched down on folded knees, but developed a problem quickly. In slow motion, he straightened to stand and rose to the top of the water again.

"I need you to come below with me," he told her when he removed the mouthpiece. "I can't reach the key under my foot with one hand while the other's cuffed to you. I'll lose my balance. If I fall over, the key will disappear in the sand again."

"It's a key, though? You're sure?" The excitement in her tone skittered across his spine in static rivulets.

"About ninety-nine percent sure. If it doesn't belong to this stupid game show, it's a key from a lost pirate ship." He grinned. "Either way, it's a win-win situation for us."

Her mouth opened in a wide O, but he held a hand up before she could shriek her delight. "Don't let on," he ordered in a soft voice. "Not until we have the key in our hot little hands."

She set her fins to float alongside his and slid her mask over her face. "Let's go."

"Slow now," he advised. "Move too fast and the key will slip away from us. One, two," he placed his snorkel back in his mouth, and she did the same, "three."

He plunged beneath the surface again, his eyes watching Renata follow him down. When they both crouched on their knees, he placed his cuffed hand on her thigh for extra support and slid his right hand beneath the ball of his foot. His fingers touched the hard metal object and, with painstaking precision, removed it from the thin layer of sand. He held the key before her, and she gave a thumbs-up as they shot back to the surface.

Flipping off the mask and snorkel, she let out a loud yell of triumph. "We did it. We really did it. Oh my God, I can't believe it. We found one!"

Lost in the excitement of the moment, she flung herself into his embrace. He wrapped an arm about her waist to keep her there as long as possible. So this was how it felt to hold a goddess, he thought. A wet goddess, but a goddess nonetheless.

Burrowing his face in the juncture between her shoulder and her neck, he licked at the beads of moisture he found there. They tasted slightly salty from her perspiration, yet clean and sweet from her very nature.

He moved his mouth from the sweetness of her throat to the confection of her lips. Nothing mattered but Renata. She was here, warm, and open to him as a flower opens its petals to a bee. The sun reflected off the water's surface and shot up, burnishing them in a blinding white light.

"You getting all this, Earl?" a voice shouted.

He snapped away from her as if on a bungee cord. There were four of them. Three cameramen and one assistant stood no more than five feet away. Filming the two of them during this very intimate moment. The white light he'd assumed was the sun, in reality came from the hand-basher in the assistant's fist. When the eight-hundred-watt bulb continued to shine in his face, he raised a hand to shade his eyes from its brightness.

"Do you mind?"

"Oops," the assistant said, flicking off the handheld light. "Sorry about that, chief."

"Don't you have anything better to do with that camera than stand around and film us right now?" Renata demanded.

"No, ma'am," the assistant replied with a smirk. "That's what we get paid for."

Her eyes spat fire at the idiot. Gone was the butter-scotch syrup Connell had always found so damned allur-ing. In its place simmered molten lava, waiting for a vic-tim to cook alive. "Well, find someone else to annoy with that thing. Or I'll find a new storage place for it. Connell, you and I should get back to shore with our key. Our teammates are counting on us."

When she turned to him, clearly expecting a reply, he managed a choked, "Right."

Wow, very eloquent, you moron. You'd better get a grip. And fast. If you lose control of your senses every time you and Renata are close, you are in a boatload of trouble, my man.

But the cameramen had made a deeper impression on his psyche than he realized. He still wanted Renata more than he'd ever desired any woman; more than he needed air to breathe. But now he knew it had to be perfect between them.

A goddess deserved heaven, nothing less. And she'd have her heaven if it killed him. Because he'd die before he lost control of himself again with an audience around them. Baptizing his solemn promise, he crouched down, allowing the water to cover him from head to toe. Steeped in his vow, he rose to face her.

"Let's go, sweetheart. We're only half done here. With any luck at all, our key fits the treasure chest lock."

They partly swam, partly waded to shore where Clarice and Gilly waited with the key they'd found.

"It's no wonder you two have to be dragged out of your tent every morning and can't wait to climb back inside every night," Gilly remarked with a knowing grin. "I don't think I've ever seen a couple so much in love as you guys."

Connell cast a glance at Renata to see her reaction to Gilly's comment. But she accepted the accolade with grace and absolutely no hint of discomfort. "I guess Connell and I were just meant to be together," she said with a shrug.

No hesitation, no quick denial, no excuses or apologies offered to Gilly and Clarice for their sudden display of passion in the lagoon. Even now, her hand remained clasped within his, relaxed and effortless. Trust. She trusted him. He'd start with that, accept it, consider it a victory. The rest might fall into place later.

Along with twelve other couples, Renata and Connell made the trek from the shoreline of the lagoon into the forest where the treasure chest hid. A couple on the Diamond Rattlesnakes team currently headed to Home Base, disappointed but resigned to their fate. The others, having found their keys, now had to find the chest hidden somewhere nearby.

"I feel like I've joined the circus," Roger complained as they pushed vines and elephant ear leaves out of the way.

"Hide-and-seek, scavenger hunts, balancing acts, what trick will they dream up next?"

"Leaping through flaming hoops of fire maybe?" Gilly suggested, eliciting a giggle from his wife.

"Or how about forming a giant pyramid atop a beach ball?" Connell offered.

"Please." Roger held up a hand in surrender. "Don't give these television moguls any ideas."

"C'mon, Rog," Trish wheedled. "It hasn't been that bad. At least we're still in the running."

"Yeah, but running where? I'm beginning to envy the couples at Home Base. For the next three weeks, they'll stay in a four-star hotel with all the comforts of twentieth-century living."

"Indoor plumbing with a working shower," Clarice said with a wistful sigh. "And a salon nearby so I can get a perm. My hair's nappier than Brillo at this point."

"Mmmmm," Jennifer agreed, a dreamy smile covering her normally pinched features, "a hot tub and lots of bubbles."

"Room service," Bruce interjected. "With entrees that don't contain fish and rice. Steak, lamb, pasta, veal. Even chicken would be a welcome change."

"Barbecued chicken," Gilly clarified. "With sauce so thick, it sticks to your fingers as well as your ribs."

"And wine," Trish added. "Or better yet, champagne."

Renata shook her head and leaned toward Connell. "This is stupid. Thinking about what they're missing is only going to make them miss it more."

"I know," he agreed in the same soft tone. "Let's just stick to finding the damned treasure chest."

"What are you lovebirds whispering about now?" Gilly called. "You two are unbelievable. You probably don't even mind the handcuffs since you're always joined at the hip anyways."

Good-natured laughter erupted from their teammates, but Renata's face burned hotter than the noon sun. She wished Gilly would stop making comments about some imaginary attraction between them. They'd found a new comfort with one another in the last few days, that's all. Not attraction or love. Simply comfort. They genuinely liked being together; they were friends, which was certainly more than a lot of other couples had going for them.

With a sigh, she turned her attention to searching for the treasure chest. If she'd waited a moment longer, she would have walked past it. A hollow log lay across her path, and the sun's burning rays glinted off the brass lock. "There it is!"

Instantly, they all rushed forward with the Bennetts and MacAllisters reaching the chest first. They pulled it out of the log, and the two couples each grabbed an end to carry it to the campsite. Racing ahead, Roger and Trish blew furiously on a whistle in a prearranged signal to the other teams that the chest had, at last, been located.

"Hurry up," Clarice urged. "I'm dyin' to see who has the right key."

"Me too," Jennifer said.

"Well, you'll have to hold out a little longer." Renata huffed and puffed beneath the heavy weight of the chest. "This thing weighs a ton."

"Really? What do you think is in it?"

Clarice leaned forward to look closer and nearly upended Renata with her curiosity when their feet tangled together. If it weren't for Connell's quick grab, Renata might have wound up face-first in the dirt and lichens on the jungle floor.

"Clarice? Could you look at the chest later, please?"

"Oh, sure." The Iowan glanced down at the ground in embarrassment. "Sorry."

"You okay?" Connell asked her when Clarice had moved on.

She nodded; the chest required too much strength to expend any on something as meaningless as talking. The muscles in her arms tingled, alerting her to their exhaustion.

As usual, he seemed to sense her predicament and murmured, "Hang in there, Rennie. We're almost at the campsite."

Staggering the last few steps, she made it into the circle in the center of the tents. When Bruce called out, "One, two, three, let her down easy," she did just that.

The moment she stood upright again, pins and needles shot through her arms. Before she could say a word, Connell's hands massaged her affected limbs, rejuvenating her tired muscles.

"Well done!" Bart exclaimed as he stepped into the middle of the clearing and put his foot atop the chest. "Now, we'll test your keys. Since the Bali Llamas found the treasure chest, we'll begin fitting your team's keys into the locks until we find who has the proper one."

Clarice and Gilly stepped forward and inserted their key first. With a loud click, the lock popped open, granting them immunity for the remainder of their time on the island. As the lid flipped open, the contestants crowded around to peek at the treasure inside. Sand. Lots and lots of sand.

Renata barely noticed. Their chances of winning the million dollars had just become a little slimmer. Like the treasure chest, they might have pinned their hopes on a foundation of sand.

Chapter Fourteen

For the next five days, the temperature soared above one hundred degrees during the day, cooling off to a balmy ninety-five at night. But the game show must go on. So it did, with teams participating in relay races, tightrope walking, and a tug of war over a murky, mosquito-ridden swamp.

By the sixth day of excruciating heat, several contestants didn't have the energy to contend with silly games. Bart Meadows and his ever-present whistle insisted they must compete or return to Home Base. His order gained grudging cooperation. Then he produced blindfolds.

This challenge began with the production assistants leading blindfolded couples by the hand. Based on the posture of his spine, Connell sensed they moved upward to higher ground. But where they headed, he had no clue. At long last, they stopped, and the familiar drone of Bart Meadows pierced the quiet.

"Now for the fun part."

Connell felt Renata lean close to him. "There's a fun part to all this?" He snickered in reply and squeezed her hand.

"Gentlemen, the PAs will remove your blindfolds. Sorry, but you ladies must keep yours in place."

"Naturally," Renata retorted.

Connell waited in the dark until he felt a tug on the back of his head. When the blindfold fell from his eyes, the sun penetrated his retinas, leaving him unable to see for a good five minutes. With the help of a few tears and some constant blinking, his focus finally returned. He found himself standing before the cavernous mouth of a dark cave.

"Ladies, I hope you trust your husbands," Bart announced, "because they are about to escort you through a labyrinth. They are not allowed to speak to you as you make your way through this mystery place. You may scream to your hearts' content, but under no circumstance is a male voice to reply or describe anything that happens inside these walls. And I feel it only fair to warn you, little surprises could pop up at any time."

Renata stiffened beside him. "Connell?"

He knew what she wanted to know—no doubt what every woman here wanted to know—where they were and what they faced. "Don't ask," he murmured. "Trust me, and you'll be okay."

Bart cast a scathing glare. "The vow of silence begins now. And since they're so eager, the Bali Llamas will go first."

With a sweep of his arm, he stepped aside to allow Gilly and Clarice past him. Connell, holding Renata's icy hand in a tight grip, followed. The moment he stepped inside, he said a silent prayer that Renata's blindfold remained in place. In setting up this little challenge, the television wizards had come up with their most heinous game to date.

Bats. They were everywhere. Hanging from the rock

ceiling above their heads, clinging to the walls around them, everywhere but on the ground.

Renata stiffened though she didn't speak a word. A twinge of gratitude went through him that he couldn't tell her where she walked right now. Because as frightened as she probably felt of the unknown, the reality of her surroundings would only terrify her more. He also understood how much fortitude it took, and how much blind faith, to allow him to guide her through this maze of walls and wings. Clarice, on the other hand, had no such self-control.

"Gilly? What's that smell? I don't like this. Not one bit. I'm gonna remove the blindfold. I don't care what it costs me."

"No, Clarice," Renata finally spoke. "Stay calm. Don't you see? They want to frighten us. That's the whole idea. They want us to come running out of whatever this smelly hole is, screaming and yammering, only to find out we've been in a safe place all along. They want us to look like fools. Don't give them the satisfaction."

"So what should we do?"

"How about we sing a song? Something light and fun?"

Immediately, Connell tickled the palm of her hand in a secret signal. How much noise would it take to wake these nocturnal creatures? And what would happen then? He tried to remember the things he'd heard about bats, all the myths versus the facts. They had a keen sense of hearing and sharp eyesight, despite the old "blind as a bat" adage. Did they bite? No, not that he could remember. And they only flew into people's hair in the movies, right?

"We must sing softly, girls," she said, and Connell squeezed her hand to tell her she was on the right track.

"W-what should we sing?" Clarice asked. "I'm too afraid to remember any songs."

"How about 'Old MacDonald'?"

"Well," Clarice's voice was still hesitant, but a little less shaky. "Okay. Old MacDonald had a farm . . ."

Connell found it the most bizarre experience of his life to date. While a chorus of blindfolded women sang every nursery rhyme they could think of, their husbands led them through the room of sleeping bats. Still it didn't end. The deeper they went into the cave, the darker it became. Soon he couldn't see a shadow around him. Connell only discovered the stream of stagnant water when he stumbled into it, splashing the slimy stuff all over Renata's calves. Her pitch rose an octave for a brief second, but she never screeched, and never gave any indication to the other ladies that she found anything amiss.

In the next recess, bats gave way to insects—millions of them. Beetles, spiders, and oversized cockroach-looking critters skittering so quickly, they gave the optical illusion that the walls were actually moving. This was the purest form of hell.

Disoriented from the blindfold, Clarice extended a hand in an effort to steady her equilibrium, and her screams of terror punctured his eardrums. "It's fuzzy, oh God, I touched something fuzzy! What was it? Gilly, where are we? When is this going to be over?"

Lucky for Gilly he couldn't tell her she'd put her hand smack-dab in the center of a tarantula nest.

In an apparent effort to calm Clarice before she sent the others into hysterics, Renata called, "Come on, ladies, don't give up now. Keep singing."

Around another corner Connell saw a sliver of white light. He gave Renata's hand a series of squeezes, and she understood the message. "We're almost done, girls. It's almost over."

Connell practically pulled her the last few feet, and the moment they reached the outdoors again, he gave her a great big hug. Thanks to Renata's clever idea, not one woman gave up, and none of the men had to utter a sound.

"I have to hand it to you ladies," Bart told them when all the couples successfully exited the cave. "You should be very proud of yourselves. If you'd like, you may remove the blindfolds to see what you just escaped."

"Take off my blindfold," Renata ordered him.

Uh, no. If she saw what Bart had just done to her, she'd lunge at the idiot and strangle him with her bare hands. And he'd be hard-pressed to stop her. Hoping to avoid such an outcome, he tickled her palm.

"Relax, Connell," she said. "I have no intention of finding out where I really was. I know it wasn't as easy as I made it sound, and I'd just as soon forget. Right now, I merely want the scarf off my eyes. It's giving me a headache."

Before he could make a move, Bart interjected once again. "Gentlemen, you may now feel free to speak, if you're so inclined."

Connell's face split into a wide grin as he untied the knot holding the blindfold over Renata's eyes. When the scrap of silk fell to the ground, he wrapped his arms around her and kissed her silly. "Lady, have I told you how proud I am of you?"

"Not lately," she rejoined, her eyes blinking in rapid succession.

"Well, I'm telling you now. You are something else, and I sure am glad you're on my team."

She smiled in his direction, apparently still blinded by the sun to really see anything, but he knew the moment she recovered her focus because she pulled away from his embrace to glare at him, hands on hips, and those gorgeous eyes flashing a challenge. "Now, about those bats . . ."

By the following morning, the temperature soared past one hundred and ten degrees. Even the crew knew better than to insist upon any activities from the contestants.

"It's just awful," Clarice confided to Renata as the two couples sat in the shallow waters of the lagoon seeking relief. "Why, I hear that at least half the contestants are so sick they can't leave their tents."

"But Bart said that Maximus Productions had an available physician on call," Renata reminded her. "And that no one is seriously ill, just uncomfortable."

"Bart Meadows is an idiot," Gilly grumbled. "My cow knows more than him."

"Dr. Franklin is working as hard as he can," Clarice said, "but with so many patients laid low, it'll be hours until he can see all of them. And from what that Loretta on the River Rats team said, lots of people are real sick."

"Well then, that settles it," Renata announced, pulling the handcuff chain to bring Connell to his feet. "I'm gonna see what I can do to help."

Resentment built within her with every step she took away from the beach. She'd tried to tell Bart last night that the heat could be detrimental to the health of the contestants, but he wouldn't listen. He just kept insisting Maximus Productions had everything under control and while things might look dire from her perspective, the network would never allow any serious harm to come to them. Like a moron, she'd believed him. She assumed they'd do anything to avoid any kind of legal action, so she'd blindly allowed Bart to pull the wool over her eyes.

Well, no more. Paying no mind to anything but the burgeoning anger filling her head, she dragged Connell straight to the idiot's air-conditioned trailer at the edge of the campsite, climbed the stairs, and pounded her fist against the door until he appeared. "Yes?"

She didn't beat around the bush. When she held up her cuffed wrist, Connell's naturally followed suit. "I'd like you to have someone remove our handcuffs please."

Bart's perfectly waxed blond eyebrow arched in a questioning manner. "Why?"

"I'm not saying it to get a break," she snapped. "I'm a registered nurse. But I can't help Dr. Franklin treat the contestants if my hand is bound to my husband's."

The dullard merely shook his head. "The only way you can be released from the 'Bonds of Matri-money' is to quit the competition. If you choose that alternative, you may treat all the contestants you wish. But once you've finished with your Clara Barton routine, you'll have no choice but to return to Home Base and await the outcome of the game."

She opened her mouth to retort, but Connell beat her to it. "Fine. Then Renata and I will do what we have to together."

"Whatever floats your boat." Bart shrugged as he closed the door to the trailer.

"Idiot!" Connell ambled down the metal stairs two at a time, forgetting Renata still chained to his wrist.

She stumbled after him, scraping her ankle on the edge of one of the stairs. "Connell, wait." His pace slowed, but he didn't stop. "Wait, please! I want to ask you something."

He finally stopped when his feet touched the ground. "What?"

She pulled up short next to him. "Do you really think you could handle working with sick people? It isn't a barrel of laughs, you know. I mean, I want to help them, but I can't ask you to be a part of it."

"Why not? For better or worse, in sickness and in health, remember?"

"Yeah, but I don't recall the marriage vows saying anything about caring for a *stranger* in sickness and in health."

He turned away but she still managed to catch the words, "If it means something to you, it means just as much to me."

Her eyes bulged with such surprise they nearly fell out of their sockets. Until she spotted the familiar white light of a television camera in the thick foliage behind the trailer. Thank God. For a minute, she thought Connell was falling for her. And that would never do because . . . because . . . well, just because!

"Renata." Clarice's telltale twang rustled the leaves and sent a flock of mynah birds flying into the still air. "Renata, Connell, where are you guys?"

"We're over here, Clarice," she called.

The rustling leaves transformed to a low thunder as the Iowan couple clambered into the clearing with Cement-Foot Gilly in the lead. "You better come quick," he announced. "You know that couple from Connecticut, Nora and Lou Bernhard? Well, it's Lou. He's real bad off. We tried to tell Dr. Franklin, but he said we'd have to wait our turn. I'm no doctor, but it don't look good."

Concern washed over Renata in waves. This heat could produce sunstroke in no time.

Her fears must have shown on her face because Connell took one look at her and yanked forward on their handcuffed wrists. "Let's go, Florence Nightingale. Your patient awaits."

They entered the tent to see Lou lying atop the sleeping bag with his wife, Nora, kneeling by his side, her lips moving in obvious silent prayer. She looked up at Renata, eyes pleading for help. "I came back from the outhouse and found him like this. I don't know what's wrong with him. He won't talk to me. He won't even look at me."

The RN in Renata took over by instinct as she scanned the torpid man's flushed and dry face. Forgetting about everything but the ailing Lou, she dropped to her knees and placed an ear to his chest. Even by estimation, his heart rate was one hundred sixty-five beats per minute, a dangerous sign. His breathing was also far too rapid for her peace of mind. It was enough to confirm her suspicions, and she flashed a worried look at Connell who knelt beside her.

"We have to get him to a hospital," she whispered, hoping not to alarm Nora. "Fast."

"He's dying, isn't he?" the distraught woman declared, wringing her hands. "I knew it. I knew this stupid game show was a mistake. I told him we had no business being here, but he was too stubborn to listen. Now he's dying."

"He isn't dying, Nora," Renata told her, fighting to keep her voice calm. "But he does need help that he can't get out here. It's a good thing you two aren't joined right now because I'll need you to run an errand for me. I want you to find Dr. Franklin and tell him your husband is suffering from heatstroke and needs to be airlifted to the nearest hospital. The doctor should radio for a helicopter then meet us at the lagoon as soon as possible. Can you remember all that?"

Nora, her wide eyes wet with tears of fear and frustration, nodded hesitantly. "I—I think so."

"Good, go. Hurry."

With another quick nod, Nora raced out of the tent.

"Very clever, Renata," Connell said with an admiring glance. "Like those old movies where they send the expectant father to boil water when his wife goes into labor."

"This isn't a ploy," she argued. "Heatstroke is extremely serious. And until Lou can be transported to a hospital, we'll need to get him immersed in cold water to bring his body temperature down. You and I are going to carry him to the lagoon to cool him off."

Connell raised his wrist to display the handcuffs. "A little difficult with these, don't you think?"

"Not really." Swerving, she called, "Gilly? Clarice? We need some help in here."

The sound of thundering hooves preceded their entrance into the tent. "You called?" Gilly asked.

"Take Lou's feet," Renata instructed. "Connell and I will take his hands. We need to carry him down to the lagoon."

While Clarice stifled a gasp with a hand over her mouth, Gilly clucked his tongue. "I knew it was bad. Well, don't stand there gawking, Clarice. Let's get the poor guy in the water."

Renata gripped one wrist while Connell took the other and the Tompkins followed suit with Lou's ankles. "Ready? One, two, three, lift," she called out, just as she would with a patient on a stretcher in the ER.

Not expecting Lou's weight to overpower her, she nearly dropped him but Connell was there to pick up the slack. "Easy," he said, bending to keep Lou from hitting the ground.

"He sure is heavy, isn't he?" Clarice managed through gritted teeth.

"Yeah," Gilly agreed. "You'd think after eating nothing but fish and rice for two weeks, old Lou might have lost a few pounds. No such luck."

"Never mind how much he weighs," Connell grumbled. "Let's get him down to the water."

They shuffled down the sand toward the edge of the lagoon where Gilly and Clarice, in the lead, stopped.

"Keep going," Renata ordered, fear for the lifeless-looking man causing her voice to raise a few octaves. "Don't stop 'til I tell you to." After wading into the water until it came up to their waists, she nodded. "Okay, drop his feet now."

They released Lou's ankles, and Renata quickly wrapped an arm around his waist to keep him from going under, ducking her head beneath his underarm. Connell must have had the same idea. He came around from the back and slammed his forehead into her skull. "Ow!"

"Okay, Florence," Connell whispered. "What do we do now?"

"We bathe him," she replied, sinking beneath the cool water's surface and pulling Lou down with her.

For the first time since the show began, Connell took a deep breath and followed his wife's lead.

Chapter Fifteen

The helicopter blades commanded attention when they whirred above the couples, raising sand to knee-level and whipping the leaves and tall grasses with a ferocious wind. The medical chopper rose, carrying Lou and Nora to RSUP Sanglah, the only hospital in Denpasar prepared to handle severe emergency cases.

"Will he make it?" Clarice shielded her eyes from the bright sun as the chopper, emblazoned with a red cross and the block-lettered title AIR-MED, soared into the clear blue sky.

"He should," a solemn voice replied. "But if Renata hadn't sent for me when she did, he might have died." Dr. Franklin peered at Renata through his Coke-bottle eyeglasses with curious intensity. "How did you know what to do for him?"

A blush of self-consciousness crept into Renata's cheeks, and Connell hid a smile. By God, he was so proud of her! She'd kept a level head, cooled poor Lou down as best she could by immersing him in the lagoon, and won the gratitude of every contestant doing what came naturally to her.

"I'm a nurse," she told the elderly doctor. "I work at St. John of Parma Hospital in Manhattan, ER department."

"Impressive. You know, you should go to med school. You'd probably make a great doctor. You've got the instincts."

"No, thanks, I like being a nurse."

"I can't imagine why," Dr. Franklin said. "Nurses are the most overworked, underappreciated group in medicine. They work long hours and get no respect from the doctors or the patients. And the pay for their level of dedication is atrocious! Or has it changed since I retired three years ago?"

"No, it hasn't changed."

"So why do you keep at it?"

"Because it's all I ever wanted to do," she admitted in a tone so soft Connell had to strain to hear her. "Ever since I was twelve years old."

"There's a story in there somewhere," Dr. Franklin hinted.

Her eyes darted at a frantic speed toward the sweeping banyan trees, across the water, back to the faces watching her with concern, then down at the sand beneath her feet. At last, she raised her gaze to Connell, and he nodded to give her the courage to say whatever she tried to hide.

It's okay, he said through his placid expression. *Whatever it is, I'll understand.*

"When I was twelve years old," she finally said in a shaky voice, "I was in an automobile accident with my family. We were on our way home from my grandparents' house on Christmas night. A drunk driver jumped the divider and hit us head-on."

"Sweet Jesus, Renata, that's awful." Gilly's eyes bulged like a bullfrog's.

Her lips set in a tight line for a long moment, and her forehead puckered. Connell had an overwhelming urge to wrap an arm around her shoulders and protect her from her memories, but he fisted his hands. Somehow, he knew she wouldn't appreciate his drawing attention to her fears right now.

"I didn't know anything about it until I woke up in Intensive Care four days later," she continued. "Both my parents died at the scene. My brother, Ralph, and I had been asleep in the backseat. EMTs brought us to the emergency room where Ralph was diagnosed with a ruptured spleen. The doctors rushed him into the operating room, but he died during surgery. I had suffered an epidural hematoma. After cranial surgery, I stayed in the hospital for three weeks, then underwent months of physical therapy. I couldn't even attend the funerals . . ."

Her voice trailed off as she stared at the broad canopy of the banyan trees skirting the water's edge. Connell had the impression she would've crawled beneath those branches to hide if she could.

"After something like that," Clarice interjected, "I would think you'd be terrified of hospitals."

Renata smiled, but her expression held no humor, only deep sorrow, and her gaze remained fixed on the dipping tree limbs.

"I met the most extraordinary people. There was Rose, an ER nurse who had just finished her shift when my brother and I were wheeled in. She came to see me everyday, even on her days off. Then in the rehabilitation unit, I met Kelly and Christian. They were my physical therapists. The minute I was well again, I knew I wanted to help people the way these people helped me. That's why

I started Majestic Health Contracting." Her voice grew stronger, more certain. "I've never once regretted that decision. Every time a child comes into the ER, every time Connell's crew successfully constructs a ramp or redesigns a floor plan for handicap access, it's like I've given something back."

Drained, she slumped against Connell as if to absorb some of his strength. She only remained there for the briefest of moments before pulling herself up again. "Excuse me," she mumbled and turned to walk away from the group of people staring at her with expressions of remorse and admiration.

As he followed behind her, his guilty conscience chastised him in nearly deafening tones only he could hear.

Idiot! You insensitive clod! How could you be so stupid?

Every callous remark he'd made since their first meeting stung like a swarm of killer bees, and he winced when he recalled his behavior on their first night on this island. No wonder she'd pulled away from him when he tried to push their kiss too far that night. First he brought up a painful memory. No, he didn't just bring it up, he actually *teased* her about being an only child and told her how everyone with siblings envied her at one time or another. Then he pawed her like a grizzly bear. Talk about smooth. That performance might put him in the Dolts' Hall of Shame.

He couldn't imagine losing a sibling the way she had. Even Duncan had his good points. Images of a twelve-year-old Renata swam before his eyes. Scared, alone, head swathed in bandages, listening to some stranger tell her everyone she loved was gone.

Moron. Big, stupid dope! You think because you know her favorite color, you know what she needs to be happy. Thinking yourself so superior to her because you've got a family to share the holidays with. God, what a jerk you are.

While his brain continued its barrage of insults, he fought the urge to smack himself in the head by clenching his hands into fists. Fists he would have liked to punch through a sheet of plywood, if one were handy. Stupid, stupid, stupid!

He stole a glance at her profile, hoping to discern how miserable her mood had become by the set of her features. She chewed her lower lip, an instinctive action he'd learned to recognize as her outlet for anxiety.

Craning his neck, he looked back at Dr. Franklin, Gilly, and Clarice clustered around the lagoon's edge a few yards away. The trio stood like lost sheep, heads low, postures shrunken and feet scuffling in the sand. He returned his attention to the woman chained at his side, waiting patiently for an opportunity to speak to her.

"Renata," he said when they were well out of earshot of eavesdroppers. "I am so sorry. Can you ever forgive me?"

She stopped and turned to face him then, her eyes widened in surprise. "Forgive you for what?"

Like the others left behind, he stared down at his feet and absentmindedly kicked at a broken shell in the sand. "You know. All the stuff I said about how lucky you were to be an only child and about Christmas."

"Christmas? When did you say anything about Christmas?"

"Well, I thought about it," he admitted ruefully. "I was thinking how pathetic it was for you to be all alone with only a cat, and how I wanted you to spend Christmas with my family this year so you could enjoy yourself."

She smiled at him, a genuine smile with no remorse or self-pity. "That's sweet. So why should you apologize for that?"

"Because your parents and brother died on Christmas Day. I don't know how you could ever celebrate the holiday with that kind of memory. And here I was thinking you just needed a hero to show you how to have fun." No longer maintaining any semblance of control, he finally gave in to his need and slapped himself in the forehead with the palm of his hand. "God, I'm such a schmuck."

"You're not a schmuck. You didn't know about my childhood. Let's face it. We're still two strangers, regardless of our marital state."

He cocked his head sideways, trying to read her mind. "Are you sure? I mean, it's obviously a painful subject for you."

"It was a long time ago, Connell," she said with an easy shrug. "It's not painful anymore."

"But you seemed so upset when you talked about it. Not that I blame you—"

A wave of her hand stopped him in mid-sentence. "That's not what upset me. Oh, it hurts to think my parents missed out on so much of my life, and I always wonder what Ralph would be doing if things had turned out differently for him. Still, I've been lucky; I had my grandparents. They taught me to look ahead, never back. Nana always said I survived that accident for a reason. And the best thing I could do to ease any feelings of guilt was to live a life that would make my family proud."

"Wait a minute. Nana. Isn't that your cat's name?"

She didn't answer him, but started walking again, turning her gaze to the copse of trees ahead. For the moment, he allowed the question to linger unanswered and followed behind until they ducked beneath the drooping branches of the banyan. When she sat down with her back against the twisted, vine-wrapped tree trunk, he sat beside her and pulled her close enough to wrap an arm around her waist. Surprisingly, she didn't pull away.

Satisfied at her cooperation, he stared at the veil the

foliage of the banyan created. She must have hoped that the thick leaves hanging down and the clumps of roots sticking up from the ground would shield them from curious onlookers. He didn't mind. At least it was cool and shady here. And a little dark, which made it more difficult for her to see the flush of shame burning his face. After a few moments in the silence, he broached the subject again. "Now, about Nana the cat?"

"I don't own a cat. Nana's my grandmother." Her voice sped up slightly as if she needed to spit everything out before he could stop her. "I should have told you about her from the start, but I don't know, I just couldn't. I didn't want you to know. I thought maybe. . . . Well, I don't know what I thought. Lillian told me I should trust you, but—"

"But you didn't want to," he finished.

"Nana's all I have left, Connell."

Of all the emotions clogging his senses right now, sympathy wasn't among them. There simply wasn't room. Not when disappointment, self-loathing, and downright resentment ate at his insides like acid. His hopes for some sort of relationship between them had just shattered like a fallen glass. If he didn't have her trust, he could never gain her affection. And that realization struck deep.

Theirs was a temporary union. Like some lovesick fool, he'd completely forgotten the lesson he'd learned five years ago: Women were fickle and couldn't be relied upon for anything. Callous, but true. Before he could piece the shards of his emotions together, a shrill whistle pierced their hideaway.

"Looks like it's time to get back to the fun and games," he growled and pushed past the curtain of leaves. "Let's go."

* * *

"Balinese Hindus believe that spilling blood on the earth maintains a harmonious balance between the earthly world and the humans who inhabit it."

Even the severity of Lou Bernhard's illness didn't dampen Bart Meadows's enthusiasm. To Renata, he resembled a shark that smelled blood in the waters—feral and heartless. Her stomach flip-flopped while she studied those even white teeth flashing in the bright sunlight. Ratings meant more to this creep than a man's health. What kind of sick, twisted monster hid behind the bland emcee's mask?

"Thus," Bart continued, "once a year, the men in the village of Tenganan indulge in a ceremony known as 'mekare-kare.' You are all about to participate in this bloodletting sport. Each couple will be armed with pandanus leaves and a shield made of rattan."

Unable to look at the man who spoke of bloodletting so easily, Renata's attention roamed until she spotted several production assistants hurrying forward with the ugliest looking branches she had ever seen. She gasped at the sword-shaped leaves tipped with razor sharp, jagged edges. Oh, sweet saints, what perverse game did the television crew have in mind now?

"One couple will fight another couple, men wielding the weapons while the women protect their husbands as best they can with the rattan shields, until one of the men draws first blood. The winner of each contest will battle another until only one man remains unbloodied. That couple will win twenty points for their team."

"No." Renata's denial erupted without warning, soft yet firm. "No way."

Connell turned to stare at her, his face a mask of stone. "A little late for second thoughts, don't you think?"

She grabbed his hand, digging her nails into his wrist

to press some sense into him. "Connell, you can't do this. The risk is too great. I've already told you what an injury out here might mean. You could get tetanus, or gangrene, or, my God, you might just lose a limb entirely with those things."

His eyes glittered with so much spite she shrank back, terrified for his safety and confused by his reaction. She'd never seen venom emanate from him, and for some strange reason she couldn't understand, his hatred seemed directed toward her right now.

"I bet you'd love nothing more than to have me back out of this," he said in a harsh whisper. "That way, you can go on thinking all men are like Steve, that none of us can be trusted. Guess what, sweetheart? I won't give you the satisfaction." He thrust his arm out to grab one of the pandanus leaves from a production assistant.

Baffled, Renata could only take up a rattan shield and follow after him as he strode out of the crowd. Why was he so angry with her? He actually sounded insulted that she would try to stop him from this stupidity. Did he think she was casting aspersions on his manhood or something?

She shook her head. Men and their damned egos. Well, fine. If he wanted to prove some idiotic theory about machismo and slice his arm off in the process, she'd have to sew it back on when he was done.

"Is the first-aid kit nearby?" she asked.

Bart Meadows shook his head. "No first-aid kit. After the fight, the combatants will be treated with a traditional healing paste made from spices, rice-alcohol, and lime."

"Are you crazy?" she demanded. "That's like rubbing salt into an open wound!"

The emcee shrugged. "If the boys of Tenganan can handle it, so can your husband."

Renata's gaze shot to Connell, begging him to stop this

insanity. He never looked her way as he held the pandanus branch in his right hand like a dagger.

"The MacAllisters of the Bali Llamas, step into the battle circle." Bart Meadows shouted like a ring announcer at a prize fight. "You'll joust the Coffeys from the River Rats."

Sudden dread filled Renata's throat with dry sand. Mark Coffey, a high school wrestling coach, was at least six inches taller than Connell and easily outweighed him by a hundred pounds. How could she protect Connell from this giant's blows with nothing more than a bamboo pot lid?

"A few rules," Bart droned on, "before we get underway. No slicing across the face or near a man's precious midsection." Nervous laughter tittered from the crowd, but the men in the circle remained stoic, waiting, while their wives exchanged looks of horror. "Let us know when you're ready, gentlemen."

"Ready," Connell said.

Mark Coffey did the same.

Bart Meadows blew his whistle, and the fight began. Renata felt as if she'd walked into the Jets/Sharks rumble in a performance of *West Side Story* and kept expecting Natalie Wood to step up and start singing.

"Oh, my Lord. I can't watch this." Clarice's voice came from somewhere behind her, but Renata didn't turn to find the woman's whereabouts. Her focus remained glued to the man with the knife-like branch aimed at her husband's chest.

Mark's arm windmilled then arced downward, and Renata quickly hoisted the shield to block Connell's face. The minute she moved the shield away, Connell slashed, aiming for Mark's chest. Angela Coffey's upheld rattan deflected it before the leaves made contact with any flesh. Mark's next thrust came dangerously close to Connell's midsection. Renata slapped it away, but the effort sapped her.

With each parry, the rattan shield grew heavier, weighing her down with the immensity of solid steel. After all the exertion she'd expended to save Lou's life, her arm muscles screamed at this new agony. She wouldn't last much longer. Already her hands shook with fatigue, and her shoulders burned from the inside out. Sweat dripped from her forehead, stinging her eyes, and blurring her vision.

"Come on, Mark," someone shouted. "Shove it in his gut!"

"Stick it to him, Connell," another voice called.

Renata suddenly knew how the Christians felt when thrown to the lions in ancient Rome. This challenge had passed cruel and wandered into the realms of torture. Why couldn't anyone else see that but her?

Mark's next thrust missed her wrist by a whisper. "Stop it," she pleaded in a voice hoarse from exhaustion. "Please."

Blinded now, she lifted the rattan one last time, but her knees refused to hold her upright any longer. She sank into a pool in the cool sand just when a ribbon of icy-hot pain encircled her abdomen. Far in the distance, a woman screamed, then a thick blanket of black shrouded Renata in nothingness.

Chapter Sixteen

Never a religious man, Connell didn't know whether praying would do more harm than good. He sat beside his wife while Dr. Franklin saw to the nasty slice across her belly. Even to treat a serious injury like Renata's, Meadows wouldn't remove the handcuffs. Slimebucket.

She groaned, drawing his attention, and her eyelids fluttered open. When she started, he placed his free hand on her shoulder to keep her still on the floor of their tent. "Easy. Dr. Franklin's not done stitching you up yet."

"And if you move now," the old doctor added, "you'll never wear a bikini again."

"Aside from that little yellow number the other day," she mumbled, "I never wore one, so no great loss there."

She winced, and Connell's attention swerved to the doctor's fingers pulling the needle and thread through her once perfect flesh. Dr. Franklin had already told him she'd probably have a faint scar from the thorns.

Connell swallowed the lump rising in his throat. All his fault. He'd allowed his anger at her to blind him to what mattered. He should have seen her exhaustion, should have known that between the heat and her heroics with Lou, she couldn't possibly have had enough strength for hand-to-hand combat. Because he acted like a macho fool, she'd have a three-inch line running across her abdomen for all eternity.

"That should do it." Dr. Franklin produced a pair of scissors and cut the knotted black thread at the top of her thigh. "She'll need to take it easy for a few days. And sadly, I have nothing stronger than ibuprofen for the pain."

"Should we airlift her to the hospital?"

"No!" Renata's head jerked up, eyes wide and pleading. "No, Connell. Not when we've come this far. We have to finish this."

Connell shot a worried look at Dr. Franklin, who regarded Renata for a long moment then shook his head. "I don't think that's necessary, but I'll go over the rest of the challenges with Mr. Meadows to be certain nothing else of this magnitude is on the agenda. Damn fool."

Dr. Franklin looked at Connell and the chain separating him from Renata. The doctor's glasses slid down his nose, and he paused to push them up again. "I'm sorry Mr. Meadows won't unhook you two, Mr. MacAllister."

Connell shook his head. "Doesn't matter. I don't intend to leave her side anyway."

"Of course," Franklin replied with a solemn nod. "If you need anything, be sure to let someone know."

"Thanks, Doc."

He waited until the flap closed behind the doctor, counted to twenty, then turned to Renata. It didn't matter that her eyes were closed. Another minute of waiting, and his head would explode from the incriminations blasting inside his brain.

"Rennie, I'm sorry. If I hadn't been so gung-ho to prove something to you, this never would have happened."

She struggled to sit up, and he quickly wrapped an arm around her waist to support her against his own chest.

"I'll forgive you provided you don't mention quitting again. I'm not leaving this game show until they throw us out."

He sighed. "No amount of money is worth your life."

"It isn't about the money now. Well, not the way you think it is anyway. I have to do this for Nana."

"Why? Does this have something to do with making your parents proud? Winning a million dollars in some freak show?"

"Of course not. I need the money to help pay for Nana's care."

"So where is your Nana these days?" he asked. "She's obviously not at the vet's."

Her eyes scanned upward, refusing to look at him. "She has senile dementia. I put her in a nursing home two years ago."

That little tidbit of information came out of left field and slammed him hard, right where it would do the most harm, in the dead center of his chest. He'd heard horror stories about nursing homes. Didn't some news program do an exposé on the substandard care provided in a pretty popular one about a month ago? Sure. He remembered the photographs of oozing bedsores, nasty purple bruises, and glazed vacant stares the residents all wore. He stifled a shiver as he thought of what it would be like to put someone he loved in one of those places.

"The first facility I put her in was awful," she recalled with a deep sigh. "Nana didn't receive physical therapy on a regular schedule. The nurses catheterized her instead of allowing her to use the bathroom because they didn't want to have to come running when she needed them. Their idea of nutritious meals looked like slop. She didn't even receive proper bedding. Everything was gray, dingy, or just out and out disgusting. It nearly killed me to see her there."

He swallowed the nausea rising in his throat. "What did you do?"

"I took on most of the duties myself. But between schlepping back and forth to St. Mark's and juggling my hours at St. John of Parma, I just about collapsed from exhaustion. And all my efforts didn't matter anyway. Almost overnight she changed from an energetic, witty senior citizen to a decrepit old lady. I couldn't allow her to stay there."

"You transferred her somewhere else?"

She nodded. "About a year ago. It took me that long to reach the top of the waiting list. No surprise. Whispering Pines has a caring staff and the best of everything. You'd be amazed at how that simple move changed Nana. Oh, she still has bad days where she thinks I'm her mother and she's a four-year-old who wants a pony for Christmas. I don't kid myself into thinking she'll ever be the same again. But at least I know she's getting the care she deserves."

"Sounds good. So what's the problem?"

"The problem is, Social Services doesn't cover all the expenses for Whispering Pines. I pay an extra five hundred dollars a month out of my salary to keep her there. Why do you think I work the night shift? I need the salary differential. And with Steve gone, all my expenses have doubled. We always split the bills down the middle, the rent, utilities, car insurance, everything. Even if I close down Majestic Health, without Steve's income, there's no way I can continue to pay the charges for Nana's care."

Connell cupped her face to cradle her head against his shoulder, marveling at how perfectly she fit there. "I promise you," he whispered, "no matter how this game show turns out, Nana's not going anywhere. We'll keep her in Whispering Pines if it takes every last dime I've got."

Renata knew he meant it. Wasn't that why she hadn't confided in him in the first place? Because she figured he'd insist on shouldering the responsibility? But the last thing she wanted was to place her trust in another man. She couldn't afford to. Neither could Nana. Gently, she pried her face out of his hands and sat upright—no more leaning on someone else's strength. At least some things were still in her power. Others? Well, she'd do whatever it took to keep control of the others.

"Thank you," she said, staring at the tent poles. "That's sweet. But I have to work it out myself somehow."

"You've already taken on too much," he said. "Why don't you let me share some of the burden?"

"It isn't your burden to share. You're overstepping the boundaries, Connell. This is a temporary marriage, remember?"

"That has nothing to do with—"

"Why do you think you're better prepared to care for my grandmother than I am? Because you're a big strong man, and I'm just a mindless, helpless woman in way over my head? I admit I made a huge mistake in believing Steve and I had some financial happily-ever-after arrangement, and I've paid a huge price for that trust. But I've learned a lot too. I'd hook on the streets before relying on another man to keep Nana where she belongs."

"Quit fighting with me and wise up," he snapped. "Can't you see we get things done easier when we work together than when we go it alone? Look at what we accomplished with Lou Bernhard."

"My grandmother isn't part of any game show."

"I never said she was. I only want to help you. I feel—"

"Don't you dare say you feel sorry for me! I don't need anyone's pity. Least of all, yours."

"If you'd let me finish," he replied through gritted teeth, "I was about to say that I feel like you and I are in this mess together. If I can keep an old lady from being sent to a place where she'll be neglected or abused, then I'll damn well do it, whether you approve or not! And if you want to 'hook on the streets,' be my guest. But as long as I've got two arms and two legs, you won't have to do it to keep your grandmother in a place where she'll live out her days in comfort and security."

Any argument she might have made died in her throat, leaving a lump of guilt the size of a baseball. With one huge gulp, she swallowed the lump and murmured, "Thank you."

"You're welcome."

"I'm sorry I jumped down your throat. I guess the last few days have really taken their toll on me."

"On both of us," he amended, placing a hand against her cheek to set her head back on his shoulder. "And I'm sorry if anything I said over the last few weeks hurt your feelings."

She allowed him to console her, enjoying the way her head fit into his shoulder. "Trust me. Nothing you've ever said has hurt my feelings."

Except, perhaps, when you called out Annie's name instead of mine after the sweetest kiss I've ever had.

"Truce?"

"Truce."

"Good." He kissed her head with a loud smack. "Now get some rest. Something tells me our pal Meadows isn't going to laugh off today's aborted challenge. And if you want to drape Nana in pearls and lace, then you'd better be up for whatever challenge he dreams up next."

Thump-thump. Thump-thump. Thump-thump. In almost hypnotic fashion, Connell's heartbeat echoed advice Renata couldn't ignore. *Trust me. Trust me. Trust me.*

Did she dare?

Chapter Seventeen

Renata, Connell, and the other couples, linked by their ankles as well as their wrists, hobbled near the waterline. As they stumbled along, Connell scanned the beach and shore for any sign of a hidden piece of paper.

Their objective this time was to find seven letters of the alphabet based on clues given in rhyme. After the letters were found, they would spell out a word. The team that solved the word puzzle first would receive a pasta dinner that evening.

"Ain't this game a beaut?" Clarice asked as she huffed and puffed beside her husband.

"At least this time if we win, they can't chalk it up to my flat head," Renata mumbled to Connell.

"Unless you have a quick brain inside that flat head," he replied with a good-natured smirk. "You any good at word games?" He already knew the answer; he'd once watched her complete a Sunday *New York Times* crossword puzzle in an afternoon. In ink.

She shrugged. "I guess we'll find out in a little while."

"Well, I'm not," he confessed. "So this one rides on your shoulders."

He looked ahead to Bruce and Jennifer searching the shoreline a few feet in front of them. Funny. The Bennetts didn't appear to have as much trouble in this three-legged race. They managed a smooth, graceful stride, swinging their linked arms in a rhythmic motion.

"Bruce, what's our first clue again?"

" 'By the shore of the blue lagoon, a letter may appear quite soon.' "

"Do you think the guy who wrote these things works for Hallmark?"

"If he does, he should be fired," Renata replied. "So, where should we look for this stupid letter?"

"Everywhere, I suppose. In seashells, under rocks. Knowing Meadows and his crew, they hid it inside a coconut."

"At the top of the tallest palm tree on the island," she added then laughed.

The sound made his heart expand in his chest. After the chunks of guilt he'd swallowed in the last twenty-four hours, he found her joy encouraging and magical. Amazing. She could turn it on like a light switch. And like a light switch, her laughter illuminated him. He only wished he could make her happy more often. Forever might be a nice start. As close as they were physically, he didn't know how to reach her emotionally.

He tripped over Renata's extended foot for the third time and, after righting himself, turned his eyes back to Bruce and Jennifer. How did they do it? While he and Renata staggered along, the Bennetts maintained their easy gait. But then he looked at the rest of their teammates.

Clarice and Gilly didn't appear to have a problem

either. Nor did Trish and Roger. The others might each trip up every once in a while, but it wasn't the stumble-bumble pace he and Renata plundered through. Why couldn't they manage that same smooth stride? Why did they resemble clumsy buffoons, like the hippos in tutus in that old Disney cartoon? Why were they so ineffectual at something kindergartners could do with ease?

One answer came back to him, echoing through the canyon of questions in his mind. Because they weren't a real couple. Not in the true sense of the word. The others, deeply in love and promised in a lifelong bond, knew their mates so intimately that every motion became automatic. But he and Renata still tried to work independently. And that contradicted the entire idea behind this game show. So how could he and Renata gain intimacy if they weren't a real couple? Talking certainly wasn't enough.

Face it. Discovering she lied to you about Nana stung you deeper than you thought. An Italian shorthair.

He snorted. How did she and Lillian hold back their laughter after feeding him that line? But even that humiliation didn't measure up to the trust issue. She'd never confided in him. Oh, they talked all the time back home. But their discussions always centered on innocuous topics, movies they'd seen or restaurants they'd liked. They never spoke about anything important, like their families or their dreams. It all came down to a lack of trust. She'd held back a tremendous amount of private information.

Yet, hadn't he done the same? When she'd questioned him about Annie that first night, he clamped down and refused to talk. God, he would love to have that night to do over again—and not just for the intense feelings the memory evoked.

Funny, the thought of Annie didn't bother him at all these days. He actually breathed a sigh of relief that he hadn't married her. And he was honest enough with himself to admit that the woman bound to him in handcuffs was the reason his heart no longer constricted when he thought about the one who got away.

"Found it!" Trish's whoops of joy carried across the shoreline, swerving Connell's attention back to the task at hand. "It's in this old tortoise shell. A letter R."

"Nice work, Trish," he exclaimed. "Bruce, what's our next clue?"

" 'Over the hill and into the wood, a letter found now would make you feel good.' "

"P.U." He rolled his eyes and held his nose. "That stinks worse than the first. You'd think Maximus Productions could find a decent poet to do the rhymes for them."

"Yeah, well, maybe Nipsey Russell wanted too much money," Renata replied with a giggle.

"I'm glad you find our predicament so amusing, sweetheart."

"C'mon, Connell, what else can we do but laugh? Wasn't it you who said all we have going for us is our sense of humor? And we volunteered for this torture. An easy way to win a million dollars, remember?"

"Oh, yeah," he said, rounding his lips in an O of surprise, which he covered with his palm. "We've been having so much fun, I forgot."

Her giggles turned to full-blown laughter, and Connell made a new vow. He'd do whatever it took to hear that sound every day they remained here. And when they returned to New York . . .

Well, better not to think about that for now. One step at a time. Just like with this stupid game show. They had to take things one step at a time.

*　*　*

Renata picked at her rice and fish with the tine of her fork, her throat too knotted to swallow. Paradise. As long as she lived, she'd never forget that word. When she'd studied the specified letters spread out in the sand: D, R, S, E, P, A, I, A, only one word came to mind. And she'd blurted it out without thinking. "Despair."

After the laughter died down, Sharon from the River Rats team gave the correct answer with a smug grin. "Ah, Bart, I believe that should be 'paradise.'"

Oooh, that burned her up. Why did Sharon have to be so condescending about her victory? As if they'd time-traveled back to high school. Once again, the queen of the cliques made her feel like an idiot in front of a crowd. But this time, her stupidity would air on national television for the entire country's amusement. Wasn't that a terrific thought?

Anyway, who cared about a spaghetti dinner? Of all the challenges they'd faced, this was the dumbest award yet. Why couldn't winners get something meaningful rather than points and dinners? Was there a reason first prize for one of these challenges couldn't be a razor? She'd swim across the lagoon with Connell strapped to her back for a chance to shave her legs right now. The coarse stubble she felt on her calves could grate Parmesan cheese for tonight's pasta eaters.

A disgusting thought. But the idea of spoiling Sharon's dinner by scraping a brick of hard cheese over her shins was too amusing not to indulge for a little while. Too bad she couldn't actually do it.

"Let it go," Connell advised, giving her hand a quick squeeze for reassurance. "It doesn't matter. We're still winning, sweetheart."

The endearment was said in a soft caress, a gentle zephyr that prickled gooseflesh from her neck to her bristly ankles. It was the second time today he'd called her sweetheart in that tone. Almost as if he meant it. Anticipation quivered down her back, but she shook her head to pry it from her spine. Ridiculous. With all the cameras and spies around, they needed to stay on their toes.

"It probably isn't very good pasta anyway," she said, dropping her chin down on her fuzzy knees. "Not like Mario's on Mulberry Street."

Bruce Bennett clucked his tongue at her. "Sounds like sour grapes to me."

Her chin came back up with a snap. "Well, you're wrong. Think about it. Italian food in Bali? It probably came out of a can. Forgive me, but my ethnic background cringes at the thought. If you're ever in New York, go to Mario's in Little Italy and you'll see what I mean. They have the freshest pastas and their sauces are like my Nana always made—thick chunks of tomatoes, lots of garlic and oregano, a splash of red wine, delicious! Have you ever eaten there, Connell?" She looked to him for confirmation of her argument, but he shook his head. "Never? You don't know what you're missing. I'll have to take you there when we get home."

His eyes glowed within the flicker of flames from their campfire in the black forest. "I'd like that, Rennie."

"Wait a minute," Bruce interjected, raising a hand in the air. "If this Mario's is Renata's favorite restaurant, why hasn't Connell ever been there?"

Oops. *Slick move, Renata. Blow your cover, why don't you?*

"Because if you had a cook like mine at home, you wouldn't go out for Italian food either," Connell said with a cocky grin. "No one makes a pasta dinner like my Renata. Except maybe her Nana. These ladies jar their own sauce, you know. Be real, Bruce. You're a chef. Do you ever go out for anything you know you can make better at home?"

Bruce shrugged. "No. I guess that makes sense."

She hadn't realized she held her breath until Bruce's capitulation forced a deep exhale from her lungs. No one else noticed but Connell. He gave her hand another squeeze, and she squeezed back a little hesitantly. Thank God for Connell. That phrase was quickly becoming a litany for her.

"I'm sorry," she whispered.

"Forget it."

Clarice popped into the conversation. "What do you guys plan to do if you win the million dollars?"

"Why don't you start tonight's discussion, Clarice?" Connell suggested. No doubt, he did it to buy time; she knew she needed to recover from her gaffe. Why shouldn't he? "What would you and Gilly do with the winnings?"

"Ha! That's easy. Update our farm equipment. Gilly's tractor is at least thirty years old. And I'd like him to have better irrigation for the south end of the farm. Then, whatever's left over, well, we'd divvy it up. Some into a savings account for our children's future, some to our church, some to charity, wherever it could do the most good, you know?"

The others all nodded in understanding. After all, Renata thought, who didn't want to use the money where it would do the most good? Wasn't that why she wanted to win? For Majestic Health and, more importantly, for Nana. To keep Nana safe and cared for, just as Nana had always kept her safe and cared for.

Another squeeze compressed her fingers, and she

looked at Connell yet again. "Win or lose," he murmured, "Nana's not going anywhere."

How did he do it? How could he continually read her mind? Was he clairvoyant or something?

"Now, who's next?" Clarice asked, claiming attention back on herself. "Bruce and Jennifer? What would you do if you won?"

"Pay off our mortgage," Jennifer replied.

"Open my own restaurant," Bruce answered at the same time.

The two exchanged a quizzical glance, as if each wondered why the other would say such a thing, and Renata held back a smile. At least she and Connell had the same goal on this front.

"You're still thinking about that word game, aren't you?"

He broke the dark silence sometime in the middle of the night. Not that it mattered. She certainly hadn't been sleeping. Her conscience wouldn't allow her such relief. Again and again, today's disastrous events ran like instant replay during a major sporting event, highlighting her embarrassment. First forward, then back, then in slow motion. All the while, John Madden's voice chastised her idiocy, and chalk lines circled the exact moment on the play-by-play when she'd screwed up everything.

"I can't help it," she confessed, her voice echoing a teenager's pitiful whine. "I hate myself."

"Hey, stop that." His large hand ran from the top of her head down to her shoulder in a sweeping motion, comforting and protective at the same time. "I told you before, we're still winning. And that's largely due to you. You've been a tough competitor, better than any of the others. You've given your all in this thing."

He paused for such a long time she thought he fell asleep. But then his voice, tired and a little on edge, cut through the darkness again. "Now it's payback time. Renata?"

"Yes?"

"I want to tell you about Annie."

"Now?"

"Yes, now," he said. "I can't exactly talk about her during the day when the cameras are whirring all around us now, can I?"

"I'm sorry," she mumbled, sitting up so he'd know she was ready to give him her undivided attention. "I just wondered why you'd wait until the middle of the night. But of course, you're right. Go ahead."

"Gee, thanks."

Back in New York, if he'd used that sarcastic tone with her, she would have told him what he could do with himself. In no time flat. But she'd learned a few things in the last two weeks. About herself and about Connell. His sarcasm now wasn't meant in a hateful way. He simply needed a chance to gain his bearings before he dove into what she suspected was a painful subject for him. While he took a few deep breaths, she used the time to rein in control of her own discombobulated emotions.

"I met Annie about eight years ago," he began. His voice was still so soft she had to strain to hear him over the buzz of cicadas and rustle of bats flying outside their tent. "At, of all things, a wedding. One of my crewmen married Annie's sister. Annie was the maid of honor, I was an usher. We dated for over a year before our families started the pressure."

"Ah," she said. "I know it well. 'When are you two going to get married? You've been together forever. What are you waiting for? You're not getting any younger, you know.' "

"I guess you hear the same thing from Nana, huh?"

"No," she replied. "Just from well-meaning friends. The married ones, of course. They seem to think they belong to some exclusive club. They want everyone they know to join as soon as possible. Nana would never do that to me. She would've preferred I waited until I fell in love to get married." A flicker of embarrassment fanned her cheeks. "Oh, God, I'm sorry. We were talking about Annie, and I stole the conversation."

"It's okay. I like hearing you talk about your Nana. I can hear how much you love her in your voice."

The flicker burst into a full-blown wildfire. She had to get the conversation back on track before her embarrassment set the tent ablaze. "Annie, Connell. Remember? We were talking about you and Annie."

"Right. Well, I finally popped the question at Christmas. Naturally, she said yes."

"So what happened?"

"Duncan happened. Duncan had joined the Army right after high school. The whole time Annie and I dated, he was stationed in Germany. But he came home about a month before the wedding. Three weeks later, I went to our apartment in the middle of the afternoon. I'd built a four-poster bed as a wedding gift for Annie, and a few of the guys and I carried it into the bedroom. I wanted to surprise her, but I was the one who was surprised. I opened the door and found Annie kissing my brother."

"Oh my God." She reached out to clasp his hand in sympathy. "Connell, I am so sorry."

And she was. She'd expected it to be something like that, but hearing such a humiliation confirmed was worse than considering it as suspicion. A flush of shame sent shivers down her spine. How could Annie do something so disloyal? And with his own brother yet? As she envisioned how Connell must have felt at that moment, anger replaced her shame. A deep, burning, brooding rage that any woman could treat such a dear, sweet man as Connell with that level of contempt.

"Needless to say, we broke up," he concluded.

"H-how did your family react to what happened?"

"They never found out about it," he admitted. "The three of us sort of made an agreement about the whole episode. We told everyone I backed out of the wedding at the last minute because of cold feet. Annie, naturally, turned to Duncan for support, and six months later they married. At least, that's the public version. More sanitary, less incriminating."

"But, I don't understand. That makes you out to be the bad guy in this scenario. Why would you want that?"

"I'd rather be the bad guy than the poor sap."

"So because of some stupid he-man pride you'd allow your family to think you chickened out of your wedding?" she asked incredulously. "Because you didn't want them to know your fiancée was cheating on you with your brother?"

"It had nothing to do with 'he-man pride,' Renata. I didn't want a stupid mistake tearing my family apart. I couldn't put my parents through something like that."

She couldn't ignore the raw pain in his tone, ragged and rough in the musical buzzing of night. Such a sacrifice fit the Connell she'd begun to know. Look at what he'd done for her. Going along with her asinine idea to get married and appear on a game show. If he'd change his entire life to help out a virtual stranger, why wouldn't he take the blame for Duncan and Annie's behavior to protect his family?

The more she thought about it, the more she realized how lucky she was Connell turned out to be an honorable guy. She'd been so intent on finding a way to save Majestic Health, she'd legally tied herself to a man she barely knew. What if Connell had turned out to be a monster instead of a prince? What would she have done if he'd abused her?

She stared up at the point of the tent, a thousand recriminations buzzing in her head. And one very big question, as well. "Connell?"

"Yeah?"

"Why did you do this for me? I mean, why did you agree to marry me and go on this game show?"

"Because you needed me. Now go to sleep. I'm wiped." Giving credence to his words, he snuggled up against her, resting their linked hands atop his hip.

Ha! As if she could sleep with that answer swimming in the depths of her conscience. He made it sound so simple. And yet, like everything else where he was concerned, there had to be more hiding beneath the surface.

She just didn't know what.

Chapter Eighteen

By the third week of competition, the Bali Llamas remained in first place, twelve points ahead of their last remaining rivals, the Birds of Paradise.

Just when Renata thought the jungle sun couldn't get any more oppressive, the weather changed. To rain. It rained all day, everyday, and all night, every night. Sheets of it poured down from the sky to slap against the leaves, splatter on the ground and splash up, leaving little brown droplets of mud on her calves, knees, and ankles.

Moving through the campsite was like trying to walk in wet taffy. With every step, the mire sucked at her boots, making an odd, thwucking sound. Her clothing never dried; it clung to her clammy skin, causing spasms of involuntary shivers from the dampness. Cooking food became impossible; campfires went out even with the waterproof matches. Mildew clung to the interior walls of their tent in filigreed green and white blossoms that stung her nostrils with pungency.

On the twenty-second morning she stood beside Connell, ankle-deep in mud, looking out over the sodden landscape. Another beautiful day in paradise. The weather matched her mood to perfection: gray, miserable, and depressing. Through the fat blobs of rain, she cast a grateful glance at her husband. Thank God for his knowledge about pitching tents on crowns. Other contestants weren't as lucky. One couple, having moved their tent and its contents three times in as many days, gave up and returned to Home Base.

Still the rain fell, and the ground could no longer absorb the excess water. Their once tranquil lagoon, swollen from constant showers, overflowed. Most of the animals had disappeared long ago, seeking shelter in caves or treetops. But each morning, when the tide receded, giant turtles and sea snakes remained beached by the ebb, floundering on the wet sand and struggling to return to their watery home.

Renata didn't mind the turtles so much; she even helped push a few back into the surf, but the snakes were another story. She was not about to touch one of those slithery things. Just the thought gave her the willies.

And thinking of snakes brought another disturbing image to mind. Maybe it was her imagination, but since she'd asked Bart Meadows to remove her handcuffs so she might help Dr. Franklin, she felt him watching her whenever they were in the same general area. And when she caught him staring, the expression on his face was cold and calculating. If not for Connell's handcuffed proximity, the emcee's interest would have her cowering beneath her favorite banyan tree. Still, it unnerved her enough to keep her on edge in his presence.

"It's time for the next challenge."

Connell's voice intruded into her thoughts, but with images of reptiles, human and otherwise, in her head, she found it a welcome intrusion.

"What do you think they'll make us do next?" she asked with a deep sigh. "Walk backward through a rice paddy carrying ducks on our heads? Eat raw dung beetles while whistling the Star Spangled Banner? Make wings out of bamboo and old heron feathers and fly around the island?"

He chuckled. "Only one way to find out. C'mon, tiger, smile. It hasn't been that bad, has it?"

"Oh, no," she retorted, wiping the river of rain dripping from her forehead with the back of her hand. "I love being blindfolded in a cave full of bats. There's nothing more challenging than walking for miles through dense jungle with a backpack on my head. And who wouldn't be thrilled to feel a tarantula crawl from your ankle to your shoulder while you lie motionless like we did in the challenge?"

"Yeah, but we won all those challenges," he reminded her. "You have to be thrilled about that."

"When I get home, I'm going to have nightmares for months about spiders in my bed. And bats hanging from my ceiling. And bugs crawling around my—"

"Okay, so the challenges haven't been a walk in the park. But we've had some fun, haven't we? Swimming in the waters at the Gitgit waterfall, singing around the fire at night, body surfing in the lagoon . . ."

"Dueling with thorny branches and dabbing my scar with calamine lotion when it was over, climbing up out of the mud when we lost the tug of war. Yessiree, bub. Fun, fun, fun. Oh, and let's not forget, the cuisine here is superb. Sand gobies, rice, fire-smoked eel, coconuts, bananas, turtle soup—"

"Now hold on a minute. Did you know in Paris, people pay upward of ten dollars for a tiny cup of turtle soup?"

"Hooray for Paris," she snapped. "At least there, those

same people are sleeping in real beds with real walls and a real roof. They have hot and cold running water, indoor plumbing, electricity, and clean underwear to put on every morning." She stretched her arms wide, palms up. "They have umbrellas, for God's sake!"

"If it's just the rain that's bothering you," he offered with a smirk, "I'll make you an umbrella out of bamboo and old heron feathers."

Frustration whittled her spine, and her eyes filled with tears she fought to hold back. But it proved as impossible as keeping a cyclone at bay with a cardboard wall. Surrendering to the downpour of emotions choking her throat, she covered her face with her hands and sobbed.

"It isn't funny, Connell. It isn't funny at all. I can't take much more of this. Do you have any idea how much I hate being here? My skin feels like wet leather. My hair has the consistency of moldy straw. I'm a walking scarecrow. I hated the heat, now I hate the rain. I hate sleeping on the ground, regardless of the weather. And most of all, I hate Bart Meadows! He's always watching me; he gives me the creeps."

A feathery touch landed on the back of her neck, a much different sensation from the plops of rain falling there for the last five days. With a start, she looked up to meet Connell's concerned eyes. "Do you want to call it quits?"

She couldn't. Too much depended on their continuing to compete. Each day that passed brought them closer to the moment when someone would win the million dollar prize. She couldn't give up.

"No," she murmured, then, tossing her head back, repeated it more firmly. "No. I can handle whatever they dish out."

With one finger, he tilted her chin up to look into her

eyes. "Are you sure? Say the word, Rennie, and we can walk away from all of it. No matter what happens, we'll keep Nana in Whispering Pines. Nothing else going on at home is as important. If you're miserable, tell me so, and we'll go to Home Base."

With her eyes closed, she envisioned what going to Home Base might mean. They'd be clean, dry, and comfortable in an air-conditioned hotel room. Dressed in real clothes again, eating real food with real utensils, and sleeping on a soft mattress with clean linens. Foil-wrapped chocolates placed delicately on lace-edged pillows where their heads would recline later in the evening.

Her mind couldn't stop the pictures flashing through it, and she wasn't sure she wanted to, although she knew such daydreaming was foolhardy. She heard the squeal of a room service cart wheeled into their suite. The spatter of raindrops on the ground transformed to the sizzle of steaks on a grill. Her nose crinkled, hoping to smell the tantalizing aromas of marinated filet mignon, medium rare, placed beside baked potatoes heaped with sour cream and chives, sweet corn on the cob dripping melted butter, and hot fudge sundaes loaded with whipped cream and a dozen cherries on top.

At the thought of such a feast, her stomach growled in anticipation. But her maltreated skin and frazzled nerves needed attention as well. A hot bath with vanilla-scented bubbles, a glass of chilled Pinot Grigio, and Etta James crooning in the background would go a long way to making everything right in her world again. Of course, Connell would probably want a long, hot shower instead of a bath, but he'd appreciate the same wine and music. She knew that much from their late-night talks.

Once they were clean, well fed, and relaxed, they'd sink into the softness of the mattress and sleep between crisp, recently washed sheets. In any position they wished because there would be no more handcuffs to restrict their movements.

And the next day when they awoke sometime after noon, room service would reappear, this time with fluffy scrambled eggs, maple-cured bacon, pancakes, orange juice, toast and coffee. Ah, blissful coffee, rich and dark with its distinctive tangy smell and eye-opening quality.

Was it wrong to revel in such luxury, even in a day-dream? What would be the harm? But she knew the answer to that. Whispering Pines, the Bardonellis, and Majestic Health all seemed so far away. But that didn't mean they'd disappeared. Without this game show and the promise it held, the same problems still waited for solutions in New York.

"No," she said aloud, shaking her head to emphasize the point. "I'm not ready to give up. Let's keep going."

Before he could argue with her, she yanked on their handcuffs and dragged them forward. They trudged through the muck to the trailer where Bart Meadows stood at the top of the stairs, beneath an awning's shelter, waiting.

How did he have the nerve to look so smug because he had all the luxuries while the contestants wallowed in wet misery? She and Connell spent many a night coming up with revenge fantasies where they cut holes in his roof, short-circuited his electrical supply, dumped dung beetles in his food. If she didn't know it meant instant disqualification, she'd go through with one of those acts of vandalism just to see him suffer for a little while.

Bart Meadows cleared his throat with a loud, "Ahem! Your next challenge is one we call, 'Light My Fire,'" he announced in his usual genial game-show-host tone. "And here's how it works. Your handcuffs will be switched so the right hands of both spouses are linked together. With some help from the members of the production crew, each lady will climb onto her respective husband's shoulders and receive a lit torch. You gentlemen will then carry your wives to the opposite end of the lagoon. There you'll find a large statue of the demon Raksasa standing before a cave. This demon should breathe fire through his nostrils, but due to the excessive rain, his flame has extinguished. The first lady to light the idol's breath with her torch will win a staggering twenty-five points for her team."

No one greeted this challenge with enthusiasm. Connell didn't wonder why. He hadn't bluffed when he told Renata he'd take her home if she didn't wish to continue. He'd had enough fun and games. And Renata probably felt worse than he did. Most of the challenges required the women to do the strenuous parts. Until this one.

As he watched Clarice straddle Gilly's shoulders, Connell shook his head. The show's producers had the sexual maturity of seventeen-year-olds. They seemed to revel in seeing scantily clad females slathered in mud, blindfolded, or soaking wet.

Regardless of her complaints to the contrary, though, Renata had held up well through all the nonsense. For someone used to the outdoors, most of the challenges came easy. But Renata was a city girl at heart. And the memory of watching her stay completely immobile while a fuzzy tarantula crawled up her bare flesh still sent shivers rocketing down his spine. It was a testament to how much she loved her Nana that she continued struggling through after that episode.

A pity he didn't instill that same sense of devotion in her. In the last few weeks, he'd had the opportunity he'd always wanted. To get to really know Renata Moon. No, correction—Renata MacAllister. What he'd discovered was a woman worth her weight in gold. And while part of him couldn't wait to return to civilization, another larger part of him wanted to remain here with her forever. At least here, they were together. But when they returned to New York, he'd lose her. And he didn't know how he would ever breathe again.

"Oh, and did I mention the added incentive?" Bart's overexcited glee cut into Connell's thoughts like a rusty chainsaw through a brick, and he had to raise a hand to smooth the hackles on his neck. "The winning team will get to remove their handcuffs for the rest of the day."

"Hot damn!" Roger clapped. He bent low to accommodate his wife's short legs and stuck his head between her knees. "C'mon, Trish. Climb aboard, and let's get that sucker lit."

After indulging in a grin at Roger's antics, Connell turned to Renata. Poor thing. She looked like a drowned rat with her hair streaming over her eyes, and days' worth of mud caked on her arms and legs. Even so, he thought her a goddess. A goddess he wanted to keep with him forever.

Somewhere deep inside his chest, a little voice cautioned him to patience. He'd made a promise to himself, and he intended to keep it. If anything, knowing Renata the way he did now made his resolve firmer. His wife deserved a real bed and real walls and all the things she'd cried about a short while ago. And if that meant he had to wait until after the "Bonds of Matri-money" ended to show her how much she meant to him, win or lose, he'd wait. Renata MacAllister was a woman worth waiting for.

He only wished he could be assured a happy ending.

The production assistant's intrusion broke the couple's silent stares as he removed the handcuffs from their wrists with a turn of the key.

"You ready, sweetheart?" Connell asked her.

"As ready as I'll ever be," she replied with a deep sigh.

With the extra height of a fallen tree stump, Renata climbed atop his shoulders, and the assistant clamped the steel bonds on again.

"On your marks," Bart Meadows called out, glancing at the imaginary watch on his wrist. "Get set. Go!"

"Achoo!" Renata removed her hand from around her torch's flame long enough to stifle her sneeze. A second too late.

"Gesundheit," Connell murmured.

"Thanks."

She rubbed her itching nose and then quickly cupped the fire again. The falling rain would douse the torch in no time if it didn't stay protected. And if that happened, they'd have to trudge back to camp to reignite it. Two members of the Birds of Paradise had already done so, giving up on this challenge and the game. A tingle of envy ran through Renata's bloodstream when she realized that within a few hours that lucky couple would indulge in the luscious daydream she'd crafted earlier. Meanwhile, whether she and Connell won or lost this challenge, she'd be soaking wet and battling a nasty head cold by night-time. Had they made the right decision by sticking it out?

Keep your eye on the prize, she reminded herself sternly. *A million dollars.*

"Where the hell is this Roxanna statue?" Roger's demand interrupted her visions of what half a million dollars in cash might look like stacked up in her apartment.

"It's Raksasa, Roger," Trish corrected with her usual superior air. "An Indonesian demon of the wilderness."

Renata stifled a giggle when Trish tilted her chin up in her schoolteacher pose and got slapped in the face with a branch of wet leaves for her troubles.

"Looks like Raksasa has had enough of Trish's history lessons as well," Connell whispered so only she could hear.

"Ssshh!" Despite her shushing, she agreed with him one hundred percent. Trish's superior attitude grated on her nerves like nails on a chalkboard, and it gratified her to see the woman get slapped down, even if a tree branch did the slapping.

For the most part, the Bali Llamas women maintained a tentative friendship, but there was no real closeness between any of them. Clarice was fun, generous, and loving. If Renata chose one woman she'd stay in contact with after this farce ended, it would definitely be Clarice. Still, she couldn't see the two of them confiding secrets or planning weekends together. Their lifestyles were too different for them to see eye-to-eye on important matters.

Trish, meanwhile, was priggish and sanctimonious. She treated her husband and her teammates with a cool, know-it-all attitude she probably used for her college history students back in Philadelphia. During the tug of war, Trish had been the first member of their team to land in the mud. Renata still didn't know whether her tumble was due to the opposing team's strength or some silent consensus of the other Bali Llamas that Trish deserved a good comeuppance.

The fourth female, Jennifer, was far too possessive of her husband's affection. If Bruce so much as smiled at another woman's joke, Jennifer would screech like a wet hen that the other woman stay away from her man. Renata found it pathetic. If Jennifer couldn't trust her husband enough to feel secure in his affections, maybe they shouldn't have married.

She didn't know any members of the other teams well enough to call them friends. They were names and faces, the competition, the ones she had to beat to win the prize. There was only one person who understood her desperation, shared in her triumphs and commiserated with her defeats. Who would have thought that, of all the teammates she encountered, Renata would grow closest to her husband?

In some ways, it made sense. From the moment they'd arrived in Bali, he'd been her cheerleader, champion, teacher, and confidant. Every morning she woke up thanking God she had him to lean on. He'd been her strength from their very first day here. Lately, she looked forward to spending time with him, working through the challenges together, and sharing every outcome, whether victory or failure.

Oh. My. God.

When you wake in the morning with thoughts of every minute you'll spend with him, that's love. Love doesn't weaken a man and woman; it gives them strength to do things they didn't know possible.

Nana's advice regarding love and lust teemed into her brain. The realization hit her so hard, she nearly lost her balance atop Connell's shoulders. Her fingernails dug into his scalp as her fist gripped his ear to keep from falling.

"Ow!" he called out. "Watch it, will you? I need that appendage. And if you drop that torch and burn my hair, you'll personally perform scalp treatments 'til it all grows back."

"Sorry," she mumbled, but her thoughts focused elsewhere.

How did it happen? When? Could she pinpoint an exact moment? Maybe something she could cite to excuse this emotion as just temporary? But no, it wasn't that simple.

She'd learned to love him through all the mundane things they'd experienced since this game show began.

It's holding hands while doing the most mundane things . . .

She almost laughed aloud at the memory of Nana's shaky voice spouting the wisdom of the ages. Holding hands? They'd had no choice but to hold hands while doing everything except using the outhouse. Then again, how many times over the last three weeks had Connell tickled her palm to communicate some secret message? A message she understood without words? How often in the darkness of their tent had she reached to touch him while he slept? Good Lord, it was true. She was in love with Connell.

So how do I keep going, knowing he doesn't love me back?

She scanned the treetops, searching for an answer, and her eyes focused on a bright strip of red cresting over the canopy of green leaves and silver rain.

"Look!" She pointed. "That's it. We found Raksasa."

"Woo-hoo!" Connell cheered, bouncing her up and down as he ran headlong into the brush to the statue. "Renata, sweetheart, have I told you lately that I love you?"

Her heart nearly flew out of her chest. Once again, he had read her mind. Even if he didn't mean it. She knew it was the heat of the moment, or in their case, the moisture of the moment that spurred such a statement.

Before she could form a reply, Bruce shouted, "Me too, Renata. I love you too!"

"Bruce!" Jennifer screeched with her usual ear-splitting accuracy. "You'd better be joking."

"Now, honey, of course I was joking," he soothed.

For Renata, the magic had disappeared, along with her little girl wishes of love and happily ever after. Swallowing her disappointment, she concentrated her sights on the ugly horned face of the statue as they drew nearer. What a ghastly looking thing! A leonine head with upturned nostrils and google eyes, its jaws gaping to show sharp fangs and a thick outstretched tongue. When they were close enough, Renata leaned her torch toward the open mouth and stifled a rack of shivers.

"Looks like my mother-in-law," Bruce quipped, receiving another disapproving squawk from Jennifer.

"Bruce!"

"I know, I know. I'm sorry, Jenny, honey. It was just a joke." He turned toward the television camera trained behind them. "Mom, if you're watching this, you know I was only kidding, right?"

"You'd better hope she doesn't see this."

"I said I was sorry." He shifted her higher on his shoulders. "Can you reach the wick of that thing yet?"

Jennifer leaned forward, touching her torch to Renata's. The flames mated beneath the gargoyle's upper jaw, and although the wick glowed, it wouldn't ignite.

"We can reach it, but it's too damn wet to light."

"Never fear," Gilly announced, elbowing his way between Connell and Bruce. "Help is here."

"We needed the rhymes last week, Gilly," Connell said. "Right now, we need heat. The wick is too wet and won't catch."

"We could rub my thighs together for extra friction," Gilly suggested with a smirk.

"Really," Trish retorted as she and Roger appeared on the MacAllisters' left. "I hardly see how that's funny."

"Okay," Gilly said. "We'll use your thighs then."

Renata couldn't hold back her giggles if she'd tried.

And she wasn't alone. Around her, everyone burst into laughter. Everyone but Trish, who let out a shocked gasp.

"Oh, relax, Trish," Roger told her. "It's just a joke. We're trying to blow off a little steam. Let's face it, the pressure is getting to all of us."

"Especially because it looks like two of us will be going home a million dollars richer than we came," Clarice added.

A hushed silence fell over the couples, broken only by the splish-splosh of rain falling around them.

Thank God for Connell. "Well, no one's won anything yet. And we still have to get this demon's wick lit. So ladies, put your torches together and ignite that sucker."

Chapter Nineteen

The minute the handcuffs fell into the production assistant's hands, Connell announced, "I'm going for a swim."

"But," she argued, holding a palm up for the rain to splash against, "it's pouring."

"I can't get much wetter than I already am," he replied then turned to walk down the beach.

She watched him go, a sense of abandonment clutching her heart and slowing its beat to an unnatural crawl. A few hours ago, she would have welcomed his departure. But now, knowing how she felt about him, she'd hoped for a chance to probe his feelings about her. Privately.

Instead, like a typical male, he'd run away at the first opportunity. With a sigh of disappointment, she crushed the tent flap in her fist and strode inside. She sat cross-legged on the tarpaulin and stared up at the points above her head, watching the water drip down into a puddle in the corner.

See Nana, I have sense enough to come in out of the rain. I just wish my heart had as much sense as my head. You'd think I would have learned my lesson after Steve, but no. Not in enough trouble, I run right out and fall in love with Connell. Isn't that a laugh, Nana? Connell!

Nana's spidery voice echoed in her head. "So what's wrong with Connell, *innamorata?*"

Nothing. Absolutely nothing. Except that after what his former fiancée did to him, he's probably sworn off women for life. Is it me, or are all men cowards when it comes to love?

Nana didn't have a ready answer, and Renata buried her face in her hands, fighting the urge to weep. God, she was the world's biggest idiot. She and Connell had made a simple business arrangement. Now she'd gone and complicated it by falling in love with him.

"Mrs. MacAllister?" a voice called from outside the tent.

"Yes?"

"Dr. Franklin sent me to fetch you. Mr. Meadows is real sick, and the doctor needs your help."

A rush of adrenaline flooded her veins, replacing the self-pity harboring there a moment ago. "I'm on my way."

Uncrossing her legs, she rose and raced out of the tent, through the muck, past the sodden foliage and up the steps of the trailer. She knocked twice on the door and, hearing a muffled, "Come in," swung it open.

The air-conditioning slammed against her wet frame with the force of an iceberg. Drawing a breath in the frosty confines of the trailer caused knives of pain to slice her lungs. She swore she could see her breath coming out in little puffs of smoke.

"Oops, sorry about that," Bart's distinctive drone came from behind an array of reel-to-reel machines and closed circuit television screens. "I should have turned down the A/C for you. We have to maintain a certain temperature in here to keep the equipment running. How about I get you a nice cup of hot coffee? It'll warm you right up."

She smelled the coffee the minute he mentioned it. Dark roast with, mmmmm, hazelnut. God, it had been so long since she'd inhaled that inviting aroma. But she found the urge to resist temptation. If it meant drinking with him, she could walk away from coffee. She'd rather drink swamp water with Connell than make her way through a bottle of Cristal with this slug.

"No, thank you." She looked around the dimly lit interior, a sense of unease settling in her bones, and she shivered. "Is Dr. Franklin here?"

"Nope." Bart's face popped up over the wall of high fidelity equipment, tanned, clear, and smiling broadly. "It's just you and me."

"You're not ill," she accused in a throaty whisper. Taking a step back into the doorway, she poised her hand on the latch, ready to flee should he reach for her. "Where's Dr. Franklin?"

"That old coot?" he asked, stepping from behind the wall of video equipment. "Who knows? Who cares?"

She watched his eyes, cold and calculating as a cobra's, skim over her from head to toe. When she looked down and saw the wet halter clinging to her skin, she quickly covered herself with her arms. He laughed, sending a whole new ripple of shivers from her head to her toes.

"You needn't worry, Mrs. MacAllister. I'm not interested in your, shall we say, feminine attributes?"

"T-then . . ." Her teeth chattered like castanets during a flamenco dance. "W-what do you want?"

He turned his back on her to fuss with the thermostat against the far wall. "I'm offering you a business proposition, Mrs. MacAllister."

"I'm not interested." She kept her eyes trained on his movements as she used her hips to push open the door.

His reply stopped her before she stepped over the threshold. "Not even if I had you and your husband disqualified from the game for perpetrating a fraud?"

The door slammed shut again, slapping her in the backside. "What are you talking about?"

With a flourish, he pushed down the button on a reel-to-reel machine behind him. Her voice flowed through the speakers to fill the chilled air. ". . . I don't know anything about you except that I sandbagged you into marrying me just to get here."

While her jaw opened and shut several times in shock, he turned and clicked off the tape, sat on the edge of the table and flipped open a manila folder. "Renata Jacqueline Moon," he read. "Orphaned at age twelve, moved in with her grandparents, Carlo and Angelina Antonucci. Carlo died in 1995. Angelina was diagnosed with senile dementia seven years later. Angelina currently resides at the Whispering Pines Nursing Home in Center Moriches, New York. Renata married Connell MacAllister—what's this?" He lifted his gaze from the file, eyes wide with overdramatic surprise. "The Friday before the production team chose you as contestants from the crowds at the Summerhouse Hotel in Manhattan." He closed the folder and slapped it back on the table. "It's all here. The application from your checking account for automatic monthly withdrawals to Whispering Pines, Majestic Health Contractors' financial records. Shall I continue?"

She shook her head, too stunned to find her voice. He'd bugged their tent. And worse, he knew everything.

"If this were a game of chess, I'd say, 'checkmate, Mrs.

MacAllister,' " he stated, leaning forward as a macabre grin spread over his bland features.

"What do you want?"

"I want to make you an offer. What did they say in *The Godfather*? Ah, yes. 'An offer you can't refuse.' "

"All right." She folded her arms over her chest, partly a gesture of defiance and partly to get her shivers under control. "You've got my attention. Is that what you want to hear?"

"As a matter of fact, it is. But before I tell you what I have in mind, I want to warn you. What I say is not to leave this trailer. You may not tell your husband, your teammates, or any of the crew. Is that understood?"

"Do I have a choice?" she retorted.

"Of course you do. You can walk out that door right now. And I can have you and your . . . er . . . husband, escorted to Home Base. After you've been disqualified and publicly humiliated. The bus is still waiting to return to Home Base with the last of the Birds of Paradise team. You could join them. Or you could listen to my plan. I'm certain you'll agree the outcome far outweighs the sacrifice required."

She had no intention of sacrificing anything for this pond scum in khaki gear, but for now, her best plan of action would be to play along. "I'm still here."

"It's very simple," he said, rising to pace back and forth in the narrow passage between the kitchen area and the wall of surveillance equipment. "Do you recall the criteria for winning this game? I listed them on the bus ride here." He studied her the way an entomologist might study a new breed of fruit fly then answered his own question. "Of course you remember. But in case you've forgotten, let me remind you that the last criteria meant judging which couple was the deepest in love."

"And how do you propose to do that?"

His fingers toyed with a button on the reel-to-reel while his eyes hinted at his power to toy with the couples as well.

"Frankly, Mrs. MacAllister, the show has become predictable and stale. Ratings have dipped in the last two weeks, and the producers want a solid teaser that will titillate the audience at home into tuning in. You are about to become that teaser."

"Why me?"

"Because, according to recent polls, you and your husband are the favorites to win. We want to shake viewers up and make them second-guess that decision. What if Connell caught you in a compromising position with one of the other husbands?"

"A little difficult while we're handcuffed together, don't you think?"

Meadows offered her a reptilian smile. "Ah, but that's why you've been released today. We'll send the contestants on one more challenge while the handcuffs are removed. You and the spouse of my choosing will veer off-course and wind up together in a rather torrid embrace, just in time for your husband and the other missus to happen upon you both."

"And if I refuse to go along with this?"

He held his hands outward. "You'll be sent packing. Of course, you might prefer that. After all, once back in Kuta, you could have a hot bath and a decent meal. The chef at the Summerhouse, Louis, was trained at the Culinary Institute of America in Hyde Park. What would be your first meal? Real pasta, like at Mario's on Mulberry Street?"

Cockroach! If she could, she'd crush him under her foot right now.

"I can see by the look of disgust on your face that I haven't convinced you yet. Well, perhaps, if I tell you the upshot, you'll come around."

"And what's the upshot?"

"Do this for me, and I'll not only allow you to remain in the competition, I'll guarantee you and your husband go home with the million-dollar first prize. In a nutshell, it's time to test your bonds, Mrs. MacAllister."

Chapter Twenty

Connell dove beneath the lagoon's surface and remained underwater until his lungs burned. When the pain grew unbearable, he vaulted up, inhaling deeply.

"You're gonna drown if you keep that up," Gilly called out when Connell rose for the fifth time.

"I only plan to do it 'til I'm exhausted."

"I can think of lotsa better things to do to get to that state, buddy," Gilly replied with a smirk.

"So can I," he agreed, wading back toward shore. "But under the circumstances, this seemed the best option."

"Uh-huh. You and Renata have a fight?"

"No."

"So then why are you here attempting suicide while she's wandering around the campsite all by her lonesome?"

"I could ask you the same question."

Gilly shrugged. "My wife's a busybody. She saw you leave, saw Renata rush out of your tent a few minutes later, and sent me to find out what's going on with you two."

"Where'd Renata go?" He walked away from the shore

and sat on a boulder near the waterline to pull on his socks and boots.

"Beats me." Gilly followed and stood over him. "So what's with you guys?"

He looked up from his laces, making his face a complete blank. "What do you mean?"

"What do I mean," he scoffed. "I mean, from the plane ride here to now, you two have given off enough heat to spark a wildfire, even with all this rain. But the minute your handcuffs are off, you bolt like an unbroken stallion, leaving your mare unattended in the paddock. What gives?"

Connell heaved a sigh as his eyes scanned the trees around them for the familiar glaring lights of cameras. Seeing none, he turned his attention back to Gilly. "Can you keep a secret?"

"I guess so."

"Don't guess, Gilly. I want to tell you something, but I won't do it if you can't keep it just between us."

"Okay, okay." Gilly held his right hand to the sky. "I swear I won't tell a soul. What?"

"Renata and I aren't really newlyweds. I mean, I guess we are, but there's a lot going on that you don't know."

In low tones, Connell told Gilly the whole story. "If I walk away, we lose and Rennie blames me for destroying her grandmother's future. If I keep going, we might win. In which case, we split the money and get a divorce. Either way, I lose Renata."

Gilly exhaled a sharp whistle through his teeth. "I don't envy you. So what are you going to do?"

He stared at the bright sky. How could it rain so heavily, yet look so damned sunny? But then, that was indicative of his problem. Damned if you win, damned if you lose. "Keep going," he said firmly. "I owe it to Rennie."

A shrill whistle pierced the pitter-pat of rain. "Get up, buddy-boy." Gilly slapped him on the back with the force of a tree trunk. "That's our cue to get back for the next go-round."

When they returned to the campsite, Connell spotted Renata at the bottom of the stairs leading to Bart Meadows' trailer. The idiot emcee leaned his head to say something to her. She nodded then tucked her lower lip behind her upper teeth.

"Congratulations to the Bali Llamas," Bart shouted. "You've successfully defeated all three other teams in the 'Bonds of Matri-money' and have qualified for the final round of competition. Now, those to whom you are closest will become your rivals as each couple vies individually for first prize. Are you ready?"

A low, unenthusiastic, "Yes," greeted his dramatic presentation and he frowned. "I can't hear you," he coaxed.

"Yes," they all said a little louder, but without a shred of excitement.

Bart nodded, a frown etched between his cheeks. "This challenge is called, 'Alphabet Soup.' Inside the barrel to my right are various letters of the alphabet. Each of you will draw a letter. You will then be attached at the waist to separate ropes leading into the heart of the jungle. Staying on your rope at all times, follow the marked trail, and search for five items that begin with your chosen letter. For example, if you drew the letter L, you might come back with a leaf, a log, a lotus, a lizard, and a . . ." Panic spread over his face as he scanned the production crew for a hint of another L word. "A lipstick."

Gilly snickered loud enough for everyone to hear then let out a muffled, "Ow," when Clarice's elbow connected with his ribcage.

"Well, you get the idea," Bart mumbled, his face turning beet red. "Use your imagination and be clever. Place all five items in the backpacks you'll carry and return to camp. The first *couple,* not individual, to make it back with the required items wins immunity from the next challenge. The last couple to return will be sent to Home Base with the Birds of Paradise team. Remember, although you'll be separated, you'll still work as a couple. So if, say, Renata returns to camp first, but Connell shouldn't return before all the others, they would be considered the losers. Understood? Let's begin. Renata? Choose a letter."

She cast a quick glance at Connell, but his discussion with Gilly had somehow thrown off his ability to read her with any accuracy. He had no clue what she tried to communicate to him.

"R," she announced, crumpling the letter in her hand.

"Excellent!" Bart grabbed her wrist and led her to the first of the ropes lying in a straight line in the sand. A production assistant wrapped another rope around her waist and secured it to that line with a metal spring clip.

"Connell, you're next."

He fished around in the barrel until his hand grabbed a folded piece of paper. Rising, he opened it to see a capital letter blazing in red ink. "S," he told the curious group.

"Fabulous," Bart replied with a smack of his hands. "Step over here please." He walked to the third rope in the line, some forty-five yards from Renata's.

Suspicion itched Connell's neck like an army of centipedes. The more he watched his wife, the more disturbed he grew. She chewed on her lip, and deep lines etched her forehead as she stared straight ahead into the trees. Something about this challenge didn't sit well. For three weeks they'd been no more than two inches from each other every minute of the day. Now all of a sudden, Bart separated them. Why?

Clarice called out, "M," then wound up on Connell's left. Gilly with, "F," was tied at the end at post number eight. Jennifer pulled a letter "G" and stood on Connell's right, blocking his view of Renata. Bruce, letter "D" in hand, was tied next to Renata, Trish's spot was beside Gilly with a letter, "I," and Roger took the only rope left with the letter "P."

With all eight people in place, Bart climbed to the top step leading to his trailer and shouted, "On your marks, get set, go!"

Connell didn't immediately leave as the others did. He locked his eyes on Bart, hoping to discern something from those depthless orbs. But Bart merely raised a golden eyebrow questioningly, waved him off with a flick of the wrist, and opened his trailer door to go inside. Having no other choice, Connell started forward into the green darkness.

"Stone," he called as he bent at the edge of the forest to pick up a rock. He tossed the item into the backpack.

He plunged ahead, scanning the underbrush around him as best he could, but the deeper into the jungle the rope took him, the more the foliage thickened.

A crackle sound crunched up from his shoe, and he looked down to see the broken pieces of a conch. "Shell," he told the cameraman, placing that item into the backpack.

He trudged a few more yards and walked straight into a spider web. "Yecch," he exclaimed, pulling the sticky threads out of his hair and off his cheeks.

God, he hated getting trapped in a web. Thinking of Renata, he couldn't help but see it as some sort of omen. When he spotted a dead spider sitting in the remnants of silk, he dropped it in the backpack.

"Three down, two to go," he told Hal, the cameraman.

Hal nodded and gestured for them to move forward again.

Farther along the trail, he saw a tree bearing large clusters of what looked like spiny brown pears. A salak tree. He hurried forward and grabbed two of the fruits. He offered one to Hal and, receiving a head shake in reply, popped it into his backpack. That made four items. One more.

As he continued his quest for a fifth "S" item, he broke through the tender skin of the second salak with a fingernail, peeled it, and bit into the yellow pulp inside. The fruit was dry with no excess juice and he enjoyed the sweetly acidic taste, almost like a pineapple but with a crunchy texture.

His eyes moved back and forth across the ground, searching for anything that would serve to meet his quota. "Okay, Hal, what can I find out here that starts with S? Shovel, salamander, salami. That would be great, wouldn't it? A salami tree in the middle of the jungle?"

Hal snickered but said nothing. So what else started with S? Snake, star, silver, spoon, sock, scorn. Could he show Bart Meadows his scorn? Would that count? No.

But a sock would. Looking down at his feet, he laughed aloud. He sat down in the mud, unlaced one of his boots and pulled his foot out. Removing his sock, he stuffed it into the backpack, replaced the boot and tied it as quickly as he could. Looking up into the camera lens, he grinned. "Bart said to be clever. That's five. Let's head back."

It took every ounce of self-control not to run down the steep incline. And while his legs kept a steady, calm pace, his heart echoed a simple communication to the jungle around him.

I'm on my way, Renata. Please be there when I get to camp.

Recriminations threw stumbling blocks the size of boulders in Renata's path. Damn Lillian! The old woman's talk about taking risks had put her in this predicament. But Lillian had neglected to mention that once you broke out of the box, your life became a continual whirlwind of risks. Now she would take the biggest risk of her life—and destroy her husband's trust.

Bart Meadows sure knew how to bait a hook. Her options were about as appealing as three-day-old scungilli. Walk away from the game show and lose everything, or allow Connell to come upon her in a torrid embrace with Bruce Bennett and win a fortune. Either way, Connell would hate her.

She had no one but herself to blame. Lillian had seen it. Even Gilly had seen it. Why hadn't she? Why hadn't she realized she loved Connell before now? Because now, it was too late.

Her rope line suddenly veered to the right, heading straight toward a clearing where Bruce the Lecher waited to get his paws on her. No turning back now. With one last sigh of surrender, she reached down and unhooked her rope from its lead.

"I'm sorry, Connell. I had no choice. Maybe someday, you'll forgive me," she whispered to the trees as she stepped forward.

She didn't look back.

Connell was the first contestant to return. As he emptied the contents of his backpack on the ground, his eyes met those of Bart Meadows, and he flinched at the hard steel reflected there. What was he so mad about? The sock? Hey, he'd followed the rules to the letter, and Bart couldn't do a thing about it. Screw him if he didn't have a sense of humor.

"You still have to wait for your wife," the emcee reminded him in a tight voice.

Connell ignored the anger emanating from the man and shrugged. "Not a problem. She's a trooper. She'll be here soon."

But time dragged on, and Renata didn't appear. Gilly and Clarice won immunity again when they showed up in second and fourth place. Jennifer and Bruce came in third and sixth. Even lollygagging Trish, with the most difficult letter of all, showed up after an hour passed. But not Renata. Connell's concern deepened to downright fear. Where was she?

"I'm going to look for her."

Clarice wrapped an arm around his shoulder for support. "Do you really think that's necessary, sweetie? You know Renata. She probably lost track of time."

Clarice was absolutely right. He knew Renata. The way she chewed her lower lip spoke volumes. Her eyes had screamed for help. He just didn't know it. Until now.

He studied Bart Meadows' trailer. The idiot hadn't bothered to come out since Connell's return. But he didn't care about that. His mind kept replaying the last time he saw Renata. The strange interaction he'd witnessed between Renata and Bart, how Bart had used them as the example of a couple who failed, the way each couple was separated on this last challenge. None of it added up. Bart Meadows was up to something.

Hadn't she tried to tell him that? She'd complained he was always watching her, but Connell hadn't paid attention. He'd dismissed her concerns as frustration. Now, she was missing.

A claw of panic gripped his insides, tearing them to

shreds with talons of dread. He should have balked, should have refused to participate this time. He should have insisted she stay by his side. From the moment they'd said "I do," they'd done everything together. How could he leave her alone when she needed him most? She could be anywhere now. She might be injured, bleeding, or ill. She might be trapped by a wild animal, terrified and cowering.

His heart climbed into his throat, and he couldn't swallow it down. It remained in the center of his neck, pounding with fierce intensity as his pulse echoed her name in rhythmic vibrations. *Renata, Renata, Renata . . .*

No matter where she was and what she faced right now, he'd find her. She needed him. Hell, he needed her.

"We'll all look for her," Gilly announced, standing beside him, but Connell shook his head.

"No." She was his wife. He'd find her. Besides, he didn't want the others here knowing the panic he experienced. "I'll follow her rope line. Clarice is probably right, and she'll come back anytime now. Meanwhile, everyone else should stay here. I'd hate to have you all roaming around looking for her only to find out she's perfectly fine."

"You sure?"

He ignored the thunderous heartbeat in his chest and muffled the lightning bolt of guilt slicing through him. What if he couldn't find her? Should he let them all split up and look for her? No. His instincts told him she wanted him to find her. He didn't know how he knew it, but he did.

"Yeah, I'm sure. I'll find her in a flash."

Picking up the end of her rope, he attached his own spring clip, still dangling from his waist, and returned to the jungle. He hadn't gone far when he noticed the strange direction her rope took. His own rope had led deeper and higher with each step he took. But hers seemed to go in a giant semicircle, leading into a small clearing near the lagoon.

"Renata!" he called. The only thing he heard in reply was his call echoing over the raucous cries of the starlings.

When he reached the end of the rope, mentally and physically, he removed his spring clip from the lead and stood for a long moment, breathing in the moist air and trying to figure out in which direction she might have gone. If she'd continued along the path, she'd have been linked to someone else's line somewhere near this clearing. Traveling uphill would take her deeper into the forest. Without a lead, that would be a foolish and dangerous thing to do. No, he doubted she'd continue on in that direction.

To the west lay nothing but denser jungle. With no trails to follow, she'd get lost among the elephant ear plants and dracaena in no time flat. Plus her fear of wild animals would keep her from entering areas the television crew hadn't properly secured. No matter what was going on in her stubborn flat head, she wouldn't needlessly risk her life.

That left one alternative. To the east lay the lagoon and the copse of banyan trees on its shoreline. The copse where she'd told him the truth about Nana. The copse that shielded them from prying eyes and zooming camera lenses. Of course.

Without hesitation, he chose the east and on trembling legs, ran in that direction. Cold rain and even colder sweat poured from his temples and down his back as he raced out of the jungle, through the clearing, and toward the low-slung banyan. He fell twice, face-first into deep puddles of muddy water. But he hoisted himself up and hurried on, never stopping to wipe the slush off his face.

The moment he reached the copse, his heartbeat accelerated to the speed of a jackhammer pounding through concrete. Taking a deep breath, he pushed the leaves aside with fisted hands to shove his head between the dripping branches . . . and came face to face with a pair of golden eyes glistening in the darkness.

Like a marionette with his strings suddenly snapped, Connell fell to his knees with a thud. Cresting waves of relief crashed over him, flooding his body. "Oh, God, Renata."

He wrapped her in his arms and placed her head against his chest, stroking her hair, assuring his frazzled brain she was real. She was safe. "Have you been here the whole time?"

He felt her nod, and he pulled her away to see her face. She'd been crying; her tears left silver streaks on her dirty cheeks, and he caught one on his fingertip, absorbing it into his own skin. In some strange way, he silently hoped it might somehow seep a trail into his blood. To stay there forever, a part of her living deep inside him.

"You threw the challenge on purpose, didn't you?" Again, she nodded. "Why?"

She didn't answer for a long time. But finally, her shoulders heaving with sobs, she tilted her head to look at him. "Bart Meadows knows all about us," she said in a husky whisper.

"Oh? And what exactly does he know?"

"Everything. He knows about our marriage, the lawsuit against Majestic Health, Nana, and Whispering Pines. He knows everything."

He laughed, and the sound released all the pent-up fears and worry from his heart, leaving him lighter and more carefree than he'd felt in eons. "You know what? I don't care. It doesn't matter what he knows, Renata. All that matters is you're safe."

"It's not that simple," she replied.

Beneath the sheltering boughs of their banyan tree, she told him all about the threat he'd made and the promise of the million dollars if she went along with his little catch-the-naughty-wife-in-the-act scheme. Connell listened to her halting explanation, anger and thoughts of violence rising from his gut with every detail.

"You wouldn't have actually slept with Bruce, would you?"

"God, no!"

"So then why didn't you go along with it? If all you had to do was feign some kind of passion between you and Bruce to see how I'd react, why not?"

Those gorgeous eyes remained fixed on his face, unwavering and certain. "Because love means more to me than money."

Love. She said love. "Love, as in 'Bruce loves Jennifer'?"

She shook her head, her smile lighting up the darkness with the brilliance of diamonds. "As in 'Renata loves Connell.'"

If he hadn't already been on the ground, he would have fallen at her feet. Hallelujah she loved him! But this time, he wanted no misunderstandings to crop up later. "You're sure? You love me?"

"Yes."

A simple enough reply, yet it filled him with such joy, such pure elation, it rendered him speechless. His mouth descended on those beautiful lips, cutting off whatever else she might want to say. He didn't want words right now. He wanted Renata. To touch her, to wrap himself around her and never leave.

Her arms encircled his neck, drawing him closer, until

their bodies pressed together, sending crisp currents of electricity through his bloodstream. They crackled and snapped, filling him from head to toe with an incredible feeling of being home. And thinking of home . . .

He broke away from her mouth, but his fingers drew a line from her luscious lips, down her jaw to her throat. "Are you ready to return to Home Base with me?"

"I'd go anywhere with you. I love you, Connell."

"Well, I'm glad you finally wised up." He grinned as he placed a kiss upon her forehead. "I love you too, Rennie."

She pulled away and smiled. "Before we go home, there's one last thing we have to do."

"What's that?"

"Short-sheet Bart's bed."

He tossed back his head and laughed. God, she was the funniest woman he'd ever known. She'd made this hell seem like a month in an amusement park. Taking her hand, he pulled her to her feet and wrapped an arm about her waist. "Let's go home."

Chapter Twenty-one

The room service cart, laden with the remnants of filet mignon, baked potatoes, and corn on the cob, sat neglected in the middle of the room. From the sound system nearby, Etta James sang her soulful ballads, and her rich coffee voice filled the suite with music of longing and fulfillment.

Blissful at last, Renata surrendered to the pleasures around her. Paradise. She finally understood the word's meaning.

Leaning against the back of the tub, she closed her eyes and sighed in contentment. Whirlpool jets eased every aching muscle in her back and legs through their pulsating vigor. With all the languor of a spoiled housecat, she lifted the glass of chilled Pinot Grigio to her lips and took a long sip. Its sour-sweet taste tickled her tongue and effervesced near the roof of her mouth. Tilting her head, she allowed the cool liquid to slide down her parched throat. Condensation dripped from the wine flute's stem onto her chest, and she placed the chilled globe of the glass against her cheeks.

After weeks of being wet and overheated, it was odd to revel in the same atmosphere here. But it wasn't quite the same. In this white and gold tiled bathroom, she had the comforts she'd been denied the last month; indoor plumbing, electricity complete with air-conditioning, a ceiling and walls, shampoo and a razor. And after availing herself of all those luxuries, she felt like her old self. Everything was the way it was before she'd heard of the "Bonds of Matri-money." Well, almost.

Feathery strokes caressed her shoulders above the churning water's surface, and she opened her eyes to look into the freshly shaven face of the man she loved. She now had Connell, who stood outside the tub, wrapped in the hotel's thick terrycloth robe, massaging her tired muscles. Even if he hadn't turned out to be a magnificent masseuse, she would have intended to keep him for life. She couldn't imagine a day, an hour, a minute without him beside her.

They had a tough road ahead. But on the long bus ride back to Kuta, they'd made a few decisions.

Connell would refinance the mortgage on his townhouse. They'd sublet her apartment. She'd work double shifts at the hospital. They'd borrow money from his family to keep Nana in Whispering Pines. It would be difficult, but they'd manage. Together.

"Any regrets, sweetheart?"

She smiled and took a deep breath as his fingers moved up to the base of her scalp in that same methodical motion. "None. I have everything I need right here."

With shaking hands, she placed the wineglass on the tile floor beside the tub.

"God, Renata, you're beautiful."

His mouth rained kisses on her shoulder. Pleasure frissoned like water droplets to roll downward, settling in her very core.

Connell leaned down to catch her earlobe in his mouth, then whispered, "Do you know how long I've waited to show you how much you mean to me?"

Renata stared into Connell's eyes, finding adoration and desire. His lips, slightly chapped from their time in the jungle, still beckoned her to taste their depths.

"Don't wait any longer," she murmured as she leaned closer, her lips pursed.

Soft as a butterfly, she landed on that luscious mouth. He tasted of the same wine she'd drunk, but along with sweet and sour, her tongue detected another flavor, spicy, like cinnamon.

As she surrendered to the undertow of pleasure dragging her beneath passion's surface, Renata's last conscious thought was, like Etta James, she and Connell were in heaven. And moving to whisper in his ear, she sang along with the final line of Etta's most famous melody.

"For you are mine, at last."

In the morning, when he opened his eyes and felt the pillow beside him, he found it empty. And cold. He sat bolt upright, dread permeating his every pore.

"Better jump in the shower, sweetheart," her voice called from the bathroom. "We have to be downstairs in an hour."

His muscles sagged back into a relaxed stance. "For what?"

She came out of the bathroom fully dressed. After all their time eating fish and rice, the silk blouse and beige slacks she'd worn on the plane swam on her skinny frame. But if they kept eating the way they had last night, her clothing would fit her again in no time.

"What are you smiling at?" she asked as she glided across the carpet toward him.

"At the incredibly beautiful woman who is my wife."

"Mmm. Lucky dog. Come on. Today's the vote," she reminded him. "We have to go back to the campsite to vote for the winning couple."

"Who cares?" He rolled over onto his side and flipped the blanket to invite her in.

She sat down on the edge then pressed her lips to his temple. "I do. And if it's important to me, it's important to you. Remember?"

"You only think it's important to you. Give me five minutes, and I'll make you forget all about some silly vote."

"I'll give you five minutes," she purred in his ear, then rose back to her feet. "You've got five minutes to get out of that bed and into a shower or I'm going without you."

"I thought this was going to be a fun honeymoon," he grumbled, but his grin belied his displeasure. "Okay, I'll get up and do what you want. But before I do, say it."

Her eyes glistened like topaz as she leaned forward and told him, "I love you."

The moment the words left her lips, he climbed out of the bed and wrapped her in his arms. His mouth claimed hers, tasting her, breathing her in until she went limp. Only then did he pull away. With great delight, he watched her sway on her feet, fighting to regain her composure. He smiled when she blinked back the clouds of passion that filled her eyes.

"I love you too."

When she and Connell stepped into the campsite, everything looked different. Their tent still stood on its little crown, the lagoon looked as tranquil and inviting as ever, and the three remaining couples still wore their jungle attire. Familiarity scratched at Renata's brain, but didn't really gain access. That is, until Clarice came running from the other end of the campsite.

No longer handcuffed to Gilly, she pulled Renata into a squeeze a boa constrictor would envy and exclaimed, "Oh, sweetie, I was *so* worried about you! Are you all right? What happened? Gilly told me some ridiculous story about you and Connell only getting married to get on the game show, and I came right out and told him, 'Now, Gilly-boy, you stop making up such wild tales. Anyone can see that Connell and Renata are just meant for each other.' I don't think I've ever seen a couple so much in love as you two. Does it bother you that you didn't win? I mean you look pretty happy right now, so maybe everything's okay. It is, isn't it? 'Cuz I wouldn't want you to be mad at me or anything. After all, it's only a game, even if it is for a million dollars—"

"Enough, Clarice, let her go," Gilly shouted. "You're gonna strangle her if you don't talk her ear off first."

When Clarice finally released her death grip, Gilly's eyes skimmed Renata from head to toe. "So you and Connell chose love over money. Wise choice. He's one hell of a guy, Rennie."

"I know," she said, tucking her hand into Connell's. "And he's all mine."

"Ladies and gentlemen," Bart Meadows' voice slipped between Renata's spinal discs like a sharpened screwdriver. "If you'll all assemble over here by this barrel, please? We will now begin the voting process. You must choose a winner between Bruce and Jennifer Bennett, Roger and Trish Gardner, or Gilbert and Clarice Tompkins. Does everyone remember the criteria?"

A chorus of "Yes," erupted in the clearing.

"One couple at a time, you'll enter that tent right there," Bart said, pointing to a large white tent covered in clear plastic tarps. "You will then discuss your vote before our cameras: who you plan to vote for and why. If you and your spouse were to get into a lively debate because you disagree about your choices, so much the better."

Yeah, sure, Renata thought. Segue right in to the next reality show, "Trouble in Paradise," where newlywed couples on a tropical island come to fisticuffs over money awarded to someone else.

Bah. Let them fight. She already had her prize. Like a warm bath, love infused her from head to toe. How had she managed to get so lucky? As if reading her mind, Connell turned his gaze to her. He smiled, mouthed, "I love you," then lifted her hand and kissed each knuckle one at a time.

"Once you've decided on a couple," Bart's voice broke the spell, a pin through a soap bubble, "you will write down your votes and place them in the barrel located directly next to the writing table. We'll tally the votes publicly so that there is no dispute regarding the winner. Let's begin."

Several of the couples rose from their fallen log seats and attempted to brush the moisture off their backsides.

"We'll start with the members of the River Rats, followed by the Diamond Rattlesnakes and the Birds of Paradise. As the losers from the Bali Llamas, the MacAllisters," Bart fairly sneered the name, "will be the last to cast their vote."

Renata didn't care how much venom he laced when he spoke of them. She fully believed in karma and the idea that Bart would one day find himself in a worse situation than the one he'd tried to manipulate for her and Connell.

After about a half hour, the last of the Birds of Paradise left the voting tent. Renata shared a glance with Connell. It was their turn. Hands clasped, they strode into the tent and faced the camera setup behind the writing table.

"We cast our vote for Clarice and Gilbert Tompkins," Connell said while Renata wrote the names on the paper. "Two people who not only taught us about friendship, they taught us the true meaning of love. Go get 'em, Gilly!"

Displaying the paper for the audience at home, Renata added, "We love you both."

Having finished, they walked out of the tent and gathered with the rest of the couples to await the outcome.

While a drum banged some rhythmic version of a ticking clock, Bart entered the tent. He returned a moment later, shaking the barrel that held all the votes. "Our couples have made their preferences known. May I have the contenders here beside me, please?"

The three couples broke from the crowd and stood, fidgety, beside Bart and the barrel that held their fates. The drumbeat continued, echoing all the contestants' heartbeats.

Without further ado, Bart reached into the barrel and pulled out the first ballot. "We have one vote for the Gardners."

Trish's face broke into a sunny grin, and Roger actually had the audacity to flash a thumbs-up at the nearby cameraman. But their happiness didn't last. As the tally continued, they only received two additional votes out of the next fourteen.

With one ballot left inside the barrel, the contest was tied with seven votes for Bruce and Jennifer Bennett and seven votes for Gilbert and Clarice Tompkins. The air grew thick with anticipation. One vote left. Who would walk away from this game a winner? And who would join the others?

Thump-thump, thump-thump, thump-thump . . .

With his usual overly dramatic flair, Bart reached into the barrel and pulled out . . .

Nothing.

"I have an idea," he said suddenly, dropping the barrel to the ground beside him. "Bruce and Jen, Gil and Clarice, at this very moment, you both have a fifty-fifty chance to win the million dollars. Or, to walk away with nothing. But what if I were to sweeten the pot for you?"

The couples looked at one another then back to Bart, their expressions cloudy with confusion.

Bart smiled with all the warmth of a crocodile. "What if I were to offer all four of you the opportunity to split half a million dollars instead? Right now. Before the last ballot is on record. Choose a safer option and a guarantee that you'd go home with money in your pocket. Two hundred fifty thousand dollars for each couple. What do you say, gang? Would you like to take some time to think about it?"

Renata exchanged a stunned glance with Connell. Yowza. This was definitely an option worth considering. After all, what fool would simply walk away from a guaranteed two hundred fifty thousand dollars?

"No way!" Bruce shouted.

Ah, of course, Renata thought. *That* fool.

"It's all or nothing, Bart," Bruce continued. "I don't even need to think about it. I'm here for the million, not some piddly two hundred grand."

"Oh God!" Jennifer wailed and slapped her hands over her face.

Chapter Twenty-two

"Let me do this slowly, okay? It's going to be a huge shock, and I'm never sure how she'll react when greeted with something she doesn't expect."

Connell nodded as he stood in the hallway of Whispering Pines Adult Home. In his hands, he clutched a bouquet of purple asters and golden mums sprinkled with dried statice. He looked at his feet and mumbled, "Maybe I should wait here while you break the news to her."

The flowers rustled against their green paper wrapper, and Renata hid a smile. Her husband was nervous. She'd never seen him so uptight before. All because he was about to meet Nana for the first time. Goodness, she hadn't been this intimidated when the entire MacAllister clan descended upon them at the airport. If she could handle hugs, tears, and kisses from dozens of eager new faces there, he could deal with one sweet little old lady here. With a cluck of her tongue, she grabbed his wrist and dragged him into the doorway. "She doesn't bite. Now come on."

Nana sat in front of the window, embroidery hoop on her lap. Her needle moved in and out of the aida cloth in slow, deliberate stabs.

"Nana?" Renata said as she pulled Connell inside the room. "It's me."

"Is it Thursday, *innamorata?*"

"No, it's Sunday. I was on vacation and couldn't come on Thursday." Bending to kiss Nana's cheek, Renata silently prayed this information wouldn't send her into hysterics.

"You went on a vacation? Good, I think you needed it. You looked tired the last time I saw you. Did you have a good time?"

"I had the best time." She flashed a knowing grin at Connell, then sat and clasped Nana's papery hand in her own. "How are you feeling today?"

In her normal routine, Nana took a pair of child's blunt-tip scissors from the pocket of her paisley housedress and clipped the threads. After unsnapping the hoop, she folded the cloth into a white square. She placed all her sewing articles inside the basket lying like a loyal sentinel at her feet.

"Wonderful now that I'm seeing you," Nana replied. "I miss you when you don't come for our visits." Her eyes lifted from the wicker basket to Connell standing in the doorway, and she winked at Renata. "Is he for me? Did you bring me a souvenir?"

Renata laughed. "No that's my souvenir. Connell, come over here." He fairly scuffled across the floor, like a little boy about to be chastised by an angry parent. "Nana, I'd like you to meet Connell MacAllister. My—" she reached up to give his hand a squeeze of reassurance, "husband."

Nana's cloudy brown eyes opened wide in surprise. A

smile spread over her heavily lined face as she reached a shaky hand toward him. "You married my little girl?"

"Yes, ma'am," he murmured. He thrust the flowers at her as if they were a burnt offering to a violent war god. "Here."

"She wanted you to take her hand, silly!" Renata chastised.

Nana didn't seem to mind. She looked from the bouquet to the man who'd given it to her, then to her granddaughter seated on her bed. "You love my Renata, yes?"

His reply held no hesitation. "With all my heart."

"Then come give me a kiss and tell me how you two met and when you fell in love." He leaned to kiss her cheek as Renata had done, and she smiled. "Mmmm, he smells nice."

"I know." She patted the bedside and Connell sat down, taking her hand within his.

"Your grandpa had a nice scent to his skin. Not like this."

"From his tobacco," Renata interjected. "Black cherry."

"I do believe you're right," Nana said. "But let's talk about that later. Right now, I want to hear about you and this handsome gentleman you brought me. Tell me everything."

"It's a long story," Renata advised.

The old lady's shoulders rose up and down. "Don't hedge. Tell Nana, and when you're through I'll give you a present."

In a halting voice, she explained everything that had happened in the last several weeks. ". . . We didn't win the million dollars," she concluded. "But we gained something far more valuable than money. We found each other, Nana. And we've never been happier."

"Who won the money?"

"A very nice couple from Iowa," Renata replied. "Gilbert and Clarice Tompkins."

She didn't add that the Tompkins had offered them one hundred thousand dollars, claiming they were a cause worth donating to. But she and Connell had turned them down gracefully. It would cheapen the love they'd discovered if they took money they hadn't rightfully earned.

"Are you angry with me, Nana?"

"Why would I be angry? You found love, didn't you?" She shook a bony finger at them. "But I would have liked to see your wedding. And you should have married in a church. It makes me wonder if I shouldn't keep the gift I have for you."

Regret stabbed Renata when she thought of the beautiful needlepoint work of a stone bridge looking over a garden at night. It would have been perfect for their bedroom. She sighed. "We understand. We're sorry. But it all happened so fast."

"You could make it up to me by having a church wedding now," the old lady wheedled. "Then I could see it for myself."

"We can't."

"I waited thirty years for this. I want to see my little girl in a white gown with flowers everywhere and a reception with all your friends around you."

"We can't afford a big fancy wedding."

Nana nodded in understanding, but her tight-lipped frown mirrored disapproval. "Well, then, I'll just give you your gift, and that'll be that."

Even after all these years, Nana could make her feel small with that look. "I'm sorry. Really I am. But we just can't do it right now. Maybe if things turn around in a year or so—"

Nana nodded again. "It's all right. I'm not angry. Connell, you look like a big strong boy. Hand me my sewing basket, please."

Connell reached down and lifted the wicker basket from Nana's feet to place on her lap. Nana opened the lid. "Your grandfather and I planned for this our entire lives. When your parents died, we decided then and there we would do everything we could to keep you safe and happy until the day you married. Hold this." She handed skeins of thread and pieces of aida cloth to Connell. "You never wanted for anything, did you?"

"Of course not," Renata replied. "You and Grampa gave me everything. I could never ask for more."

"That's good to know." With a gleam in her eyes, she pulled a large metal box from the bottom of the basket. She dropped the basket on the floor and placed the box on her lap. One hand reached inside her blouse to pull a sterling silver chain up over her gray head. Behind the Miraculous Medal she wore lay a silver key. It took a few minutes for her trembling hands to open the lock, and in the meantime, the silence in the room was deafening.

She probably has a hundred needlepoint pictures stored in that little box for us.

But when Nana flipped the lid open, Renata stared in amazement. Cash, lots of it! Hundred dollar bills wrapped in rubber bands stored neatly in even little piles inside the battered metal box. "Nana! Where did that come from?"

"From your parents' life insurance policies," Nana replied then turned to Connell. "Did she tell you about the accident that took my Camilla and her family away?"

Connell nodded solemnly.

"You mean you've had all this money inside your sewing basket for eighteen years?" Renata's voice rose as she lifted one of the wrapped bundles with trembling hands.

"You know Grampa never trusted banks," Nana reminded her. "When your parents died, *innamorata,* you were so ill for such a long time. Grampa received the money about six months after the accident. We put it in this box, and we swore we'd never touch it. It was for your future. We thought if we couldn't afford your college education, then we'd use some of this to pay. But you got your scholarships and between that and the little bit your Grampa and I put aside, we didn't need it. Grampa and I agreed this money was to be your wedding present. So you'd never know hardship."

"H-how much money is here?" Renata asked, too stunned to take it all in at once.

"Fifty thousand dollars."

Thank God for Connell. He grasped her elbow to keep her steady as she crumpled against his chest.

"We did it all for nothing," she mumbled in disbelief. "All the challenges, the heat, the rain. All for nothing."

"I wouldn't say it was for nothing," he replied with a grin. When she tried to argue, he brought his lips down on hers.

No, it wasn't for nothing after all.

Chapter Twenty-three

The front door to the MacAllister home opened wide, releasing a whiff of beef and a rush of warmth into the cold air on the porch. A short, buxom woman with Connell's light hair and eyes stood in the doorway. "Look who's here!" Keita MacAllister screeched as she pulled Renata into her arms.

"No hug for me, Mom?" Connell asked wryly as he stepped over the threshold and into his brother's house.

"Bah!" his mother retorted, slapping his shoulder play-fully. "You, I've hugged all my life."

"Merry Christmas, Mom," Renata said.

"Merry Christmas, my newest daughter," Keita replied, kissing her cheek.

She finally released Renata, and her gaze swerved to the two ladies behind her daughter-in-law. Renata reached for the fragile looking woman first. "This is Nana—er, Angelina Antonucci. Nana, this is Connell's mother, Keita MacAllister."

Keita leaned forward to embrace the woman warmly. "Welcome, Angelina. Merry Christmas."

"*Grazie,* Keita."

"Come on, Nana." Connell took her hand and led her out of the hall. "Let's get you by the fire."

Renata cast her husband a grateful look before turning to their last companion. "This is Lillian Van Horne." A feathery face peeked out of the top of Lillian's coat. "And Buttons."

"Ooh." Kiernan popped around the door, blue eyes wide with wonder. "Is that a real bird?"

"Why, yes, dear boy."

Lillian opened her coat to allow Buttons to fly free. For today's festivities, Buttons wore a red hat with white fur trim and a bell on its pointed top. Renata shook her head. Poor Buttons.

"What kind of bird is he?" the child asked.

"*She*'s a pied cockatiel and a very clever girl." Lillian knelt before Kiernan so they were nose-to-nose. "Would you like to see her do some tricks?" The boy nodded. "Show me where the kitchen is, and I'll let her perform for you."

"Not in the kitchen," Keita told them. "Kiernan, take Lillian and Buttons into your playroom. There's more room in there for a cockatiel to fly around."

"Okay, Grandma."

Lillian walked past Keita, dropping her coat on the woman's arm and handing her a large brass bird cage. Without a word, she followed Kiernan into the back of the house. Renata winced. Only men found themselves on the receiving end of Lillian's charm. Women were considered competition, and Lillian deigned it best to put them in their place at the outset.

"Sorry about Lillian."

But Keita patted her cheek with affection. "Don't fret. Connell already explained Lillian's idiosyncrasies to us."

She released a sigh of relief and looked around the foyer. "Where's everyone else?"

"Annie's fussing in the kitchen, Paisley and Davina are running late so I'm doing doorman duty. Take off your coat. I'll hang it while you say hello to everyone in the living room."

"Maybe I should go to the kitchen and help Annie?"

"Now, dear, trust me. Annie has everything under control. She's a regular tyrant when it comes to her kitchen. I've learned the best thing you can do is stay out of her way. Don't be insulted. She's happier when she's in control. You understand, don't you?"

"Of course."

Actually, she was grateful she didn't have to go into the kitchen. The smell of roasting meat played havoc with her stomach these days. She shrugged out of the heavy woolen overcoat, tucking her hat and gloves inside the sleeve before handing them to her mother-in-law.

Entering the living room, she first settled her gaze on Nana who sat near a roaring fire, a dreamy smile on her face, a handmade afghan tucked around her legs and a glass of Drummond MacAllister's world famous eggnog in her hand.

"Connell!" a deep voice bellowed from the kitchen.

Duncan MacAllister appeared in the living room, Lillian right behind him. "Renata," Duncan said, "would you please tell your friend that I absolutely cannot have a cockatiel in my house?"

Renata smiled. She'd been prepared to dislike Duncan and Annie for what they'd done to Connell. But when she met them at the airport after their return from Bali, she saw right away that these two belonged together. Tiny, bird-like Annie thought the sun rose and set on her Scots warlord husband. Every sentence she uttered began with,

"Duncan says," "Duncan thinks," "Duncan wants." And for all his gruff mannerisms, Duncan turned into a purring pussycat with a crewcut the minute Annie so much as smiled in his direction.

"Oh, but they're much more affectionate than cats," Lillian argued, "and don't require as much care as dogs. You'll see. I never thought I'd get used to having one in my home either, but now I don't know where I'd be without my Buttons."

A screech of delight preceded the arrival of Kiernan, following the airborne Buttons. The cockatiel landed on the back of the couch and bit Lillian's jacket to gain her owner's attention. Annie, exasperation on her face, came into the living room right behind them.

"Kiernan, darling, maybe in another year or two. But Santa has come and gone this year, and I will not call the North Pole to find out if he can FedEx a cockatiel to you now."

Biting back her laughter, Renata rubbed a hand over her still flat belly and wondered whether the child growing inside her might be an imp like Kiernan or an angel like Nana. More likely, Caelan or Rhona was a combination of herself and her husband. Which meant they probably had their work cut out for them when this little one appeared seven months from now.

"Children are such a joy, but they're also a great deal of work," Annie said as she settled down in a chair near the Christmas tree.

"I'll remember that," she said.

Annie's eyes swept from Renata's bosom to her stomach, and she grinned. "I'll bet you will."

Renata exchanged a quizzical glance with her husband. She'd only told him about their pending arrival this morning. It was part of his Christmas gift; that and the gold wedding band wrapped possessively around his third finger. But they'd agreed to keep the baby a secret between them for a little while longer. So how did Annie know?

"No one said anything," Annie whispered. "I can see it in your eyes. But don't worry. I won't tell. It's your surprise, and you'll tell the family when you're ready."

"Thank you," she whispered back.

"I heard the charitable contributions for Majestic Health are pouring in faster than you can count 'em," Drummond said. "I guess the fame your stint on that game show brought about was worth something after all, eh?"

"Trust me, Dad. Fame isn't all it's cracked up to be."

"What did Andy Warhol say?" Annie asked. " 'In the future, everyone will be famous for fifteen minutes.' "

"Yeah, well," Connell replied, "fifteen minutes of that was more than enough."

"Fifteen minutes . . ." Lillian rambled as she tapped Annie on the shoulder. "Did you say my Andrew said something about fifteen minutes?"

Annie looked up at Lillian, her pretty blond brow wrinkled in confusion. "Yes, Andy Warhol said that a long time ago."

"Imagine that," Lillian replied. "My Andrew."

"Lillian?" Renata asked. "Did you know Andy Warhol?"

"Well, of course I did, sweetheart. He was the art student who painted that portrait I gave you as a wedding present."

"Wait a minute!" Duncan interjected. "Wait just one minute. Are you saying that horri—er, lovely painting—hanging in their living room is an original Warhol?"

Lillian nodded. "Do you think it's worth something? I always knew Andrew had talent, but I was never much of an art buff, myself."

"I'll be damned," Duncan exclaimed, rubbing a hand over his chin. "My brother has a fortune hanging on his wall and doesn't even know it."

"What can I say?" Connell replied with a shrug. He cast his eyes down to Renata's stomach meaningfully and murmured, "It seems like every time I turn around I'm discovering I'm richer than I ever imagined. And it's all due to Renata."

"No, Connell," she told him, drawing his face to hers. "We both gained all we could ever need the moment we said, 'I do.'"

B